BLOOD SHIPS: Secrets Untold Book One

A Novella by

Amy Blackwell

ISBN-13: 978-1-7365214-1-0

Cover design by: Aljon Inertia & The English Option
Library of Congress Control Number: 2018675309 Printed in
the United States of America

Dedication

This novella is dedicated to time. May we find truth in it.

Prologue

A friendly greeting from across the sea
Painted faces, wigs, none of them female.
Inferiority is what they see
Horseshoe-shaped token, a body for sale

Some wouldn't survive under the sky's gloam
Beautiful brown bodies dumped overboard
This ship's voyage would never make it home
Bum-rushed by masked freemen, a great horde

Painted faces, wigs, now colored in red
One by one as they kiss the ocean's floor
Tale of this ship, a mystery instead
Explorers of new land, free, masked no more

Blue waters, food, and a mouthful of hope
Members of the same tribe, Welcome to Slope.

Contents

"Sometimes you can have a whole lifetime in a day and never notice that this is as beautiful as life gets."

~The World According to Garp~

CHAPTER 1

The Guts

There was nothing like the view of the sun as it gently kissed Slope's horizon. The way the sunlight bathed the land made everything feel right, as if all was just as it should be. Slope was a place filled with good feelings, offering everything we needed to thrive. I loved it for that. But, then again, I was born here, and for those who came from elsewhere, their stories were different.

To me, Slope was the only home I had ever known and the only one I wanted to know, or so I thought. I'd heard stories about other places, but none of them impressed me with the way they fascinated Jholie. The origins of Slope intrigued me far more. For that, you could blame Meema. She was my anchor, my world within a world. There were few questions she couldn't answer, though I sensed there were some she simply wouldn't.

Meema used to tell me vivid stories about blood-streaked ships that passed through our waters, manned by monstrous-faced sailors who raided and pillaged them. Deddy would tell her to stop scaring me, but she never did, and I was never scared. He'd mutter that she was just an old woman passing the time with tales, but I believed her. Meema and I had a way of talking. Her stories wove lessons into life, even when I wasn't ready to learn them.

Slope itself looked like one of Meema's famous gumbos, full of life and flavor. People of all shades lived here: brown, black, light, yellow, and the mixtures in between, blending into something uniquely whole. We all got along, driven by the same unyielding purpose, life. Meema often said we came from the same place: captivity. I didn't quite understand what she meant, and I wasn't eager to find out. Still, I'd nod like I understood, because that was what you did with Meema. Except for a few eccentric souls, Meema called "not wrapped tight" Slope was safe. Problems, if they arose, were handled by the elders, and justice was swift. Yet, there was one person Meema often warned me about: Sara. She hadn't lived here as long as most. And how she got here, no one knew. Like my Mamma, she just showed up one day, alone. She moved through the village like a shadow, her head always bowed as though counting her steps.

Meema said it was heartbreak that weighed her down and assured me that time would mend her. I used to watch Sara as though she were a scene in one of the stories Miss Jones told us about. Her movements seemed to speak in their own way. Her eyes held a sadness that stirred my curiosity, and I often found myself wondering what sorrow she carried. Sometimes, she would walk in endless circles, lost in her thoughts. I'd sit with a piece of sugarcane, chewing as I watched, mesmerized.

There was this one-time Jholie decided to march straight up to Sara, but before a word escaped her mouth, Meema appeared out of nowhere, popped her on the behind, and marched her off to the shed.

Everyone in Slope knew what Meema's shed meant. Jholie's screams echoed through the trees like a wild boar's final cry before a pack of coyotes. They were a sharp reminder that you didn't mess with Meema.

Meema was everything wrapped in one, gentle but stern, sweet but no-nonsense, spiritual yet grounded. She often told me she talked to the "most-high," asking for protection over the land during prayer. It made me uneasy, her way of weaving spirituality with everyday life, but she stood firm in her belief.

Meema's faith ran like an undercurrent through our days, subtle yet unyielding, touching everything without ever announcing itself. She'd hum hymns while tending the garden, her voice carrying an ache, I couldn't quite understand.

It wasn't until one hot afternoon when Lilly and I used to be close friends that I finally got the understanding that I needed. We just finished playing in the pasture when Lilly and I sprawled under the shade of the old pecan tree, that I realized how deeply those whispers of faith reached through our family.

Lilly, with her wild curls and wilder imagination, picked at the blades of grass as she spoke, "Meema prays for the land, you know," she said, as if revealing a great cosmic secret. "She thinks it's alive, like us. Like it listens. Not like my Nana."

I frowned, rolling the thought over in my mind, "That's just Meema being... Meema."

Lilly tilted her head, eyes narrowing. What if she's right? What if the land hears everything we do? Feels everything?

Her words made me shiver, even in the sweltering heat. That's how Lilly was turning an idle afternoon into something that lingered in your bones.

Lilly, Micha's older sister, had her own peculiar way of seeing the world. About my age but far more dramatic, Lilly claimed that lying in the fields and letting the wind shape her face gave her divine visions. She swore she'd lived before and vividly remembered her death. She'd recount these eerie tales with a conviction that made them almost believable.

Her family was just as odd, known for their strange insights. Lilly's Nana often muttered that nothing as perfect as Slope could last forever. "Slope won't last always," she'd say, drawing Meema into heated debates. Meema would counter, saying, "Slope don' seen three generations thriving already." It was always entertaining to listen to the two of them go back and forth. Their words started out in one tongue and finished in another.

The Praiser's sermons added to the mystique of our community. His voice would rise and fall dramatically, sending chills through me as he led the People of Song in praise. Folks would stomp, shout, and sometimes collapse in a sweaty, frenzied heap as the spirit moved among them, or so Meema said. I wasn't so sure. I preferred to keep my distance from things I couldn't see or understand.

Afterward, the quietest moment in Slope came during the feast. Every mouth was busy chewing the endless array of dishes: gumbo, roasted meats, freshly baked bread, all a testament to the

diversity and abundance of our home. At
the head of the horseshoe-shaped table
sat the elders, their whispered
conversations laced with hints of wisdom
and gossip.

I always listened carefully,
pretending not to as my mother teased me
for being too nosy. But their whispers
hinted at truths and mysteries that only
deepened my love, and questions, about
Slope. Life in Slope had its rhythm, a
balance of work, play, and connection.
Even with all the quirks, heartbreaks,
and peculiarities of its people, life
always seemed to settle into something
that felt right.

After evening baths, the
neighborhood came alive again, the sound
of laughter and the murmur of
conversations carrying across the strip.
Older men gathered near the big wooden
gate with the red sign, sharing news and
passing a flask or pipe between them.
The gate wasn't used often, as plenty
came and few went from Slope, but it

stood as a reminder of the boundary between our home and whatever lay beyond it. I never cared to find out…until.

Miss Jones often hosted story time on her front porch. Children from all over the neighborhood would pile up, sitting cross-legged on the ground while she spun tales from her chair. She claimed her stories came from her great-grandmamma and were older than the trees around us.

Sometimes, her stories were about bravery, other times about monsters that prowled outside Slope. "They're just stories," Deddy would say when I'd get wide-eyed listening to her. "Don't let her fill your head with nonsense."

Meema didn't discourage Miss Jones's storytelling, though she'd warn me not to take all of it as gospel. "Sometimes folks just like to make you think," she'd say.

Of all the stories Miss Jones told, the one about the Old Willows stuck with me the most. According to her, the trees on the far edge of Slope weren't just trees. They were alive, not in the usual sense, but with spirits who watched over Slope. They swayed their heavy branches even when there was no wind, and if you listened closely, you could hear them whispering. I never got close enough to find out, though Jholie claimed she talked to them all the time.

"The tree moved," she told me one night, eyes wide and full of certainty.

"Its branches touched the ground, and I swear I saw eyes on it." I laughed at her, but I avoided the Old Willows for weeks after that.

Despite the calm that blanketed Slope, there was an undercurrent; a sense that something lingered just beneath the surface. Maybe it was in the way folks talked about what they didn't understand, or in the quiet moments when Meema's prayers carried a little extra weight. Whatever it was, I didn't have a name for it.

One evening, just as the sun dipped

low enough to turn the sky pink and gold, I sat with Meema on the front porch. She was shelling peas, her fingers nimble as they flicked each one into the metal bowl on her lap. I rested my chin on my knees, watching the horizon.

"What are you thinking about?" she asked without looking up.

"Do you ever think Slope could change?" I asked, surprised even myself with the question.

Meema paused for a moment, her hands still. "Change can come anywhere, child. But it doesn't always mean things get worse."

Her answer didn't satisfy me entirely, but I nodded anyway. A breeze swept through the porch, carrying the smell of something sweet and earthy from the fields. For now, everything felt steady.

That night, after Meema put the bowl of peas away and the lamps were dimmed, I found myself staring at the ceiling, unable to sleep. Somewhere outside, an owl hooted, and the cicadas droned in harmony. For all the mystery Slope held, there was a peace in its rhythm, a promise that for all its complexities, this was home. And for now, that was all I needed.

CHAPTER 2

The Gate

The path behind the schoolhouse was gated and marked with a red slash, glaring and bold, a warning meant to keep people like me away. The sight of it made my temples throb, a question burning in my mind. It was no warning, more like a dare to me.

I asked Meema first, why we couldn't climb the fence behind the schoolhouse. She ignored me, so I went to Mamma.

Conversations with her weren't long or deep. Mamma was more of a teacher than a mother most of the time, always looking to instill a lesson rather than share a laugh. I needed strategy to approach her, not charm.

One afternoon, when the sun blazed high in the sky, I found her at the lake's edge, washing linens. Her tune hummed softly, rising and falling like the ripples on the water. Quietly, I crept closer. Meema always said I had "feet of cotton," but Mamma had the ears of a wolf. Sure enough, she noticed me before I could say anything, casting me a fleeting glance before focusing back on her wash.

"Mamma?" I blurted, stepping into her view. "Why is the gate painted red?"

Her hands paused, the linen dripping suds into the lake. She turned to me, raising her eyebrows high. "You know why the gate is painted red," she said slowly. Her voice dipped low. "And you know to stay away from it."

"I understand," I said, fighting the smirk that pulled at my lips as my eyes darted skyward.

"Don't play with me, girl," she snapped, gathering her basket of damp linens. As she brushed past me, she stopped and turned, her gaze dark.

"Do you understand?" she asked again, her voice cutting like the wind before a storm.

"Yes, ma'am," I answered quickly, pushing my smirk away.

Satisfied, she kept walking. I trailed after her, but as we passed the gate, I slowed, unable to resist looking closer. The boards were sturdy and weathered, yet familiar. Mr. Stone made them, his signature notch in the bottom-left corner gave it away. He was the only one in Slope who left his mark like that, crafting each board as if it were sacred. At the top, jagged nails jutted out every other board, an intentional, menacing deterrent.

Peeking through a slim gap between the boards, I tried to see what lay on the other side. Before I could glimpse anything, Mamma's voice startled me.

"Don't even think about it, Bri," she barked, not even bothering to turn.

I followed her quickly, my cheeks

burning as if she'd caught me red-handed. When we reached the gate itself, I stopped, hearing the faint rattle of chains.

Wait, there it was again, unmistakable.

"What's that?" I started to say, but Mamma grabbed my arm.

"Let's go," she said sharply, her eyes scanning the gate like it might snap open at any moment.

"We gotta get back," she added, pulling me along.

We hurried toward the schoolhouse, but my curiosity stuck to me like burrs.

Outside, Linc, Gene, Bam, and Paul stood in a huddle, their voices low and faces serious.

"Mamma, I'll be right there," I called, waving her off. She didn't glance back, just kept walking. As long as I wasn't near that gate, she didn't care much about what I did.

"What y'all talking about?" I asked, joining the group.

"I heard screaming from behind the

gate," Linc said, his voice hushed. "We want to go see what's back there."

"Screaming?" I said, intrigued. "Mamma and I heard chains rattling earlier. But how're you gonna see what's back there? That fence is nailed to keep anyone out."

"How you know?" Paul asked, narrowing his eyes.

"I just do," I replied quickly.

"Y'all know if the elders catch us back there, we'll all be in for it."

"We found a way," Linc said, leaning closer.

Gene grinned. "There's a tunnel in the basement of the schoolhouse," he whispered. "It's hidden behind one of them tall shelves Mr. Stone made. That sucker's heavy, too."

"Yeah, it weighs just as much as your momma!" Gene joked. Paul shoved him. "Stop playing. We serious," Linc said.

"Well, what's the plan?" I asked, crossing my arms.

"Uh… we don't have one," Bam admitted.

"You mean to tell me y'all standing here acting like this is all figured out, and you don't even have a plan?" I shook my head.

"Waste."

"A waste of what?" Gene asked, frowning.

"BRAINS!" I hollered as I walked away.

"Are you gonna do it?" Bam called after me.

"Do what?"

"Come up with a plan?" Bam asked, her voice rising.

Frustrated as I was, curiosity wouldn't let me walk away from a good plan.

"Yeah," I said finally. "Later."

That night, the clatter of hooves pulled me from my thoughts. I crept to the window where Jholie was already perched, her wide eyes scanning the darkness. Five horses, their riders cloaked in black, rode silently past, a carriage trailing behind. I stared at the driver, her long braid swinging beneath a weathered hat—

like one of Deddy's old hay raking hats.

The group stopped near the schoolhouse, and the riders dismounted, disappearing around the side.

"Bri, don't go," Jholie pleaded as I grabbed my boots.

"I just need to see what's going on," I whispered. But when she ran to check on Mamma and Deddy, she came back with a terror I hadn't seen before.

"Mamma and Deddy—" she stammered, "They're gone! The bed's still made like it was this morning."

"What?" I froze, but deep down, I already suspected. That it was them in the group. It had to be.

The sound of horses coming down the strip towards the house startled me, again. I grabbed Jholie and belted through our room door. We swiftly jumped in our beds, threw the cover over our heads, and waited. We expected to hear the front door open but we heard nothing. Instead, the back door let out its usual squeal when it was being opened slowly. Jholie and I lowered the cover and stared at the door.

We heard Deddy's voice.

"Kibby," Deddy said. "What got into you tonight?" Deddy continued.

When Deddy called Mamma by her first name we knew it was something important going on. Jholie and I looked at each other from across the room then we heard Deddy's footsteps approaching our door. We pretended to be asleep. He looked into our room and shut the door. I tiptoed to the door and pressed my ear against it. Jholie watched from her bed.

"Baybruh, I don't know? I wanna burn that damn gate and that old barn to the ground. And everything in it," Mamma said.

"And what we gonna do bout' the schoolhouse once it starts burning, too? If we do that, we gonna have more to explain than to clean up." Deddy said softly.

"We can rebuild the schoolhouse in that back lot by the cornfields," Mamma added.

"But what about what's underneath?" Deddy whispered.

We heard the slam of their bedroom

door. I got back in bed then I got out of bed and tiptoed out of our room. I needed to hear more. I sneaked to the edge of Mamma and Deddy's bedroom door, pressed my ear against it, and listened. I could only hear bits and pieces of them talking.

Something bout' a devil woman caged up and bandits on a ship. After they finished talking, I ran back to bed in amazement. Although it was just bits and pieces of words, I couldn't believe what I had just heard.

The next morning, Mamma and Deddy were waiting for me at the breakfast table which was odd because we all ate together. There was no sign of Jholie or Meema.

"Bri, what were you doing last night?" Mamma asked.

"Nu'in' Mamma, sound asleep. As a matter of fact, I never slept better," I said and let out a fake yawn with my arms fully extended in the air.

"I am going to ask you one last time, girl. What did you hear or see last night? I know you were up. The curtain was open and the shutter was, too," she said with the look. "And after Baybruh closed your door last night, it was opened this morning," she scolded.

I sighed. "Nu'in Mamm—."

Before I knew it, she had me stretched out on my bed with her paddle. She beat me till my behind turned red. The worst part about the beating wasn't the smacks. It was the words that were coming out of her mouth with every hit that hurt me the worst.

"DIDN'T I TELL YOU NEVER TO LIE TO ME!" Mamma yelled.

The paddle whistled in the air before it connected with my backside.

SMACK! I held on to my tears.

"I'M YOUR MAMMA, YOU ARE NOT MINE. I KNOW EVERYTHING ABOUT YOU!" she continued.

The paddle whistled its high-pitched tune once again. SMACK! My tears still held tight in my eyes.

"HOW CAN I STAND UP FOR YOU, IF YOU LIE TO ME!" Mamma yelled.

The paddle song continued. SMACK! I couldn't hold the tears any longer. They came rolling down my face in bunches, but

I knew that they were not from the pain I was feeling. They were because I knew she was right. I'd severed a bond between her and me. The smacks continued to whistle until the last words came across her lips.

"I CAN'T trust you!" her voice sank with the last strike of the paddle. Smack!

I tried to mouth the words, I'm sorry, but I just couldn't bring myself to it.

The next morning, I felt different. I mean, nothing had changed physically, I just felt like I had a point to prove to Mamma, to myself, and to Slope. Being more responsible was just as important as being honest, although, I felt like not everyone deserved my honesty and everyone didn't deserve my lies.

I didn't mention the gate or the fence for a while. I even stayed in my bed when I heard the horses at night, but I never stopped paying attention to the schoolhouse and the gate. I took mental notes of the goings-on that took place around the schoolhouse and how often I heard the horses. I could tell that Mamma

and Deddy switched up their movements,
too. They were rarely gone at the same
time during the night, or so I thought.
Instead of riding the horses and carriages
down our strip, they took a different
route. That much, I could tell.

CHAPTER 3

MAMMA & DEDDY

Deddy always said I got my stubborn streak from Mamma. He even laughed one time and said, "Y'all just alike."

That's hard to believe, especially knowing how Mamma and Deddy first met. It's something nobody really talks about, and when I asked Deddy, all he said was, "Go ask your Mamma."

That was the end of it because I knew better than to ask her anything she didn't want to tell me. There was only one person who'd give me answers about their story. Meema.

Meema is Deddy's momma. She was on

one of the first ships to land in Slope.
Like me, Deddy was born here, but not
Mamma. I didn't know much more until
one quiet morning, I found Meema sitting
out in the cornfield as the sun just
started peeking over the horizon. She was
at the edge of the field, beside two stone
rectangles, rubbing her feet in the soil
and mumbling to herself.

I walked slowly through the stalks
until I stood in front of her.

"Meema," I said.

She didn't even look up.

"What, chile?"

I cleared my throat. "Can you tell me
about Mamma and Deddy?"

Her eyes rolled straight up like
I'd said the worst thing possible. "And
just why you think I'd tell you 'bout
that?" She leaned toward me. "You 'member
the beatin' you got for lyin'?"

"Yes, ma'am." I answered quickly.

"Then don't get smart, now," she
scolded. But even with all that fuss, the
morning was too nice, the sun too warm,
and the soil just the right temperature

for a good story. Meema sighed, stretched her legs in the dirt, and finally started talking.

"Back when Slope was still new, we didn't have many people 'round here," she said. "Few ships had touched these waters. Everybody knew everybody 'cause we had to. But one day, your Mamma showed up like a ghost outta nowhere. Most folks come in groups, but not her." Meema tilted her chin toward the woods.

"Your Deddy was just 'bout a man when it happened. One morning, he was out collecting kindling, when your Mamma came runnin' outta those woods, cryin' and shakin'. She was bare as the day she was born, with coal-black hair down to her bottom and cheekbones that screamed Injun blood. Skin dark like Nile queens, lips too. And her back…" Meema's voice trailed off, her face tight with something close to pain.

I waited.

Finally, she whispered, "Her back was torn up, child. Whipped bloody bad. Scars already swollen, dried blood stinking like rotten meat."

I was trying to listen, but my mind wandered. I couldn't help but think I'd never seen Mamma's naked back, not once.

Now, I knew why.

Meema kept talking. "She was carryin' this smooth, shiny stick. Came from a tree I ain't never seen before. And that stick, chile, under the right moon..." Meema paused. "That stick glows blue at night. Creepy, if you ask me." Meema chuckled to herself, the sound raspy but full of humor. "Your Deddy sure didn't know what to do, and neither did his stick."

"What you mean?" I asked, trying to keep up.

"Never you mind." Meema swatted at the air. "Anyway, she ran smack into your Deddy, and let me tell you, chile, his stick was awake." Meema raised her eyebrows and cackled.

"What does that mean?" I interrupted. Meema waved me off again. "Hush, now. Point is, your Deddy had never seen

a naked woman before, and he fell in love
on the spot. And don't ask me why,
somethin' wrong with that boy for sho'.
You see a muddy, naked woman carryin' a
glowy stick, and you think love? Creator
help him."

I laughed along with her, even
though I didn't quite understand what she
was saying.

Meema leaned in again.

"When he brought her to me, I 'bout
fell out myself. She didn't speak for
days. Got up at sunrise just to mark that
stick and slept the rest of the time till
a fever hit her bad."

"She got sick?" I asked, wide-eyed.

"But she lived," Meema smiled. "Your
Deddy made sure of that."

He marked her stick for her every
sunrise while she was sick. When she woke
up and saw what he done, she stopped
mumblin' in that strange tongue."

"What kind of talk was it?"

"Old words, chile. Words I ain't heard
since the old women from my ship spoke
'em. Your Mamma don't remember a thing,

but that don't mean she forgot. I know better. She don't forget nothin'."

"Ask her about Lynn from down the way. Betta yet, don't ask'ha. She might stretch you out again," Meema sneered.

I looked on, but before I could say a word, Meema went on.

"Everyone thought Lynn and your daddy would jump the broom, but I could tell that wasn't gon' happen the day your he seen your momma. Lynn had come over for dinner after hearing all the fuss of your momma's arrival. She wore her best dress and fixed her hair real nice. She strolled in and sat in the chair next to your daddy. Your momma came in and sat to the right of me opposite Lynn. He got right up and moved to the seat next to her. Sitting at the table, Lynn could see it too. She ain't never been back over for dinner, no'mo."

"Meema, where'd Mamma come from? Why was she runnin'? And those scars, why?"

Meema looked tired suddenly. "Not today, chile." She shook her head and added, "But I'll tell you this, your

37

Deddy never gave up. She made him work, but he won her over. That darkness she carried? He chased it right out. And then…" Meema winked. "Well, it wasn't too long 'fore you came along."

I smirked. "That's where my stubbornness comes from, huh?"

"Sure is," Meema said with a dry laugh. "Now don't go givin' them a hard time. They doin' their best, same as we all are. And they love you. Never forget that."

Our talks always ended that way. I never forgot those words.

CHAPTER 4

The Plan

The festival season has finally arrived. Winter's cold grasp was loosening, giving way to blooms that seemed to paint the world anew. Bellies were round with promise, and hope hummed in every corner of Slope. For me, this time of year was a reset, a chance for renewal in the way seasons turned. It made me wonder, could it be the season for Mamma and me to find common ground, too?

The festival buzz was a town-wide symphony, each of us a note with a role to play. Deddy commanded the horse show, and naturally, Bam, Linc, and I were part of it. Truth be told, it was Bam's show—we were her side acts. She didn't settle for less than perfection, drilling us with relentless practices from sunup to sundown. My legs ached, my arms burned, and by the time I staggered home each evening, my exhaustion clashed with Mamma's expectations. Lucky for Bam that I had a real bond with my horse.

Hadie was my favorite horse. She was a beautiful brown mare with a long black mane. She and I had a bond that folks could see by looking. I remember this one time, Deddy told me to go get five eggs from the coop for breakfast. I didn't feel like taking the walk, so I whistled for Hadie.

She came flying, full speed, right at me, almost running me over. That was one of her ways of messing with me. She finally stopped playing and walked up to my face, snout-to-nose, then grunted. She turned to her side so that I could mount her. When I took a step towards her, she sidestepped away. I took another step and so did she. By this time, Mamma started yelling at Deddy about the eggs, I could hear her from outside.

Deddy looked out of the looking hole and saw Hadie and me. He thought I was wasting time, but little did he know, Hadie was messing with me. He came storming out of the house. Hadie let out a grunt and took off, I, right after her.

She slowed.

I grabbed the saddle, swung myself onto her back while she was still in motion. Deddy watched in awe.

I rode to the coop and back with the eggs in my sack. Deddy came running out of the house. I jumped down off Hadie on her left side at the rear. Deddy gave me that look, I handed him my sack. Hadie slapped me in the back of my head with her tail.

"Thanks, Hadie," Deddy nodded and smiled while walking back into the house.

While I wrangled horses in the festival, Mamma and Meema had their own hands full. The costumes were the heart of the festival and came from their fingers. Threads spilled like rivers over the table as they stitched long into the night, heads bent and voices murmuring softly.

With both of them consumed in their work, a lot of house chores fell to me. I pressed through my weariness, managing to comb Jholie's hair, prepare supper, and fold the linens while Mamma's spirit lifted with each passing day.

In the mornings, Mamma was full of life, singing in her native tongue and tapping out drum rhythms on the back door. By the time the kitchen filled with breakfast smells, or when she disappeared into the bedroom with Deddy for a spell, she carried a glow that softened her edges.

Meema and Mamma's job was important. They sewed every piece of cloth to be worn at the festival. They got up early and stayed up late. Bam, Linc, and I were the first to try on our costumes. Our outfits had to be loose enough to move freely, but full enough to cover everything. And just as I expected, they fit perfectly.

After our fitting, Bam, Linc, and I met up on the side of the schoolhouse for practice. Bam had some crazy stunt she wanted to practice that might kill one of us by the time it was done, but she didn't care. First, she showed it to us on her horse. She mounted her horse and did a *whipty-do*, *whumpta-lump*, and *bippity-boom*.

"See, it's easy," Bam said.

Linc and I looked at each other with doubt.

"It's easy…for you," I replied.

I mounted Hadie, tried the same stunt that Bam showed us when all of a sudden, Hadie let out an excruciating neigh, and galloped right into the schoolhouse. I jumped down off her and immediately went to look closely at Hadie. I noticed that she was favoring her left hoof. There was a sharp piece of wood stuck in it.

"Bam, go get my Deddy!" I shouted. She darted toward the house as I rubbed Hadie's trembling neck.

"It's gon' be alright girl." I rubbed Hadie's neck.

I rubbed her nose then bent down to look more at her hoof with Linc right by my side. That's when it happened, a baby's cry. Piercing and raw, the sound came from the schoolhouse, where we thought no one was. Linc and I exchanged wide-eyed glances, our panic momentarily forgotten.

He rushed to the door of the schoolhouse and forced his way in when Deddy and Bam showed up. Deddy noticed the door to the schoolhouse was open right away. He hurried past Hadie and I and walked straight up to the schoolhouse door.

"Get out of there Linc. Look what you did to this doe'." Deddy complained.

"But Suh, I heard a baby crying in'ere," Linc panted.

"No you didn't, now let me see what's wrong with Hadie." Deddy walked over to Hadie, shut the door, and pushed Linc along.

"But, Deddy! There was crying. We heard a baby!" I said, my voice firm.

He acted as if I never spoke. He walked over to Hadie and raised her right hoof. He grabbed a huge metal apparatus that looked like scissors with teeth from his waistband and yanked the piece of wood

from Hadie's hoof. Hadie grunted with
disbelief.

"Hadie gon' need some rest for a bit.
If she gon' be ready for the festival,"

Deddy instructed.

Bam looked at Linc and me with
disappointment. She knew that meant no
practice for a spell.

"Don't you all go back in that
schoolhouse. I'll be back with more tools
to fix dat' doe'." Deddy looked Linc
straight in the eye then walked away.

Bam, Linc, and I huddled up.

Deddy mounted his horse, rode hard to
our house, and stormed through the front
door where he found Meema and Mamma
stitching costumes for the festival.

"Kibby, I need to talk to you, now."

Deddy shuffled through the door.

"What now, Baybruh. I am busy."

Mamma gets up from the table.

"I know Kibby, but this can't wait,"
Deddy said nervously as he marched into
the room. Mamma got up and walked in behind
him.

"She had it. Da' kids heard it crying," Deddy said frantically.

"See, I told you to get rid of her, long time ago," Mamma started pacing back and forth. "Did you go in and talk to'ha?"

"No, the kids was right dere', but somebody is gonna have to go over there and see about her." Deddy peeked out of the looking hole.

Mamma stiffened, her eyes narrowing.

"I told you to handle it!"

"I'll go later," he relented.

"But look Baybruh; we gotta get to the bottom of this. You gon' have to take it from her," Mamma wiped her forehead. "How and why would anyone sleep with…"

Mamma got frustrated.

"Hush Kibby, we've already said too much. We know we gots a problem, now we gonna have to fix it." Deddy whispered.

"Well, what we gon' do, Baybruh?"

Mamma questioned.

Deddy walked to the door, pressed his ear up against it to make sure no one was listening. Then he walked to the looking hole, slightly moved the curtain aside, and peeked from around it to make sure no one was snooping around.

Mamma hissed, "After the festival, take care of it."

"We end this." Deddy decided.

"Wait, Baybruh, what about de' one who got her in'at situation? Has he come forth?" Mamma inquired.

"No. But when he does...I'll have his head. I gotta go, de' kids are waiting on me back by the schoolhouse." Deddy marched off.

Deddy ran through the door and mounted his horse. Jholie walked slowly from the side of the house chewing on sugar cane as if she was never there.

"Deddy, can I go wi'cha?" Jholie asked.

"No, go help your Mamma," Deddy replied.

Jholie stumped into the house. Deddy rode back to the schoolhouse.

"We both know what we heard," I said.

"What did you hear?" Bam questioned.

"We will tell you later, but I got a plan to find out what's going on in de' basement of dat' schoolhouse and behind dat' fence," I whispered.

Bam and Linc's eyes bulged with excitement.

"After we finish our routine for de' festival, while everyone is busy, we are gon' meet at de' fence along de' side wi' all of de' markings. Linc, bring gloves for each of us." I pointed at Linc.

Linc nodded.

Bam looked down the strip and said,

"Yo' Deddy is coming."

"Bam, Linc, bring a change of clothes, just in case we need to…" I turned and looked over my shoulder and saw Deddy approaching.

"…change if we get dirty. Bam bring some cotton to put on top of de' fence so dat' we can climb wid'out getting our skin ripped open. I'll bring de' tools. And remember not a word to no one." I stared at both of them. Their eyes agreed.

48

"Linc don't forget to tell Gene and Paul to sound de' drum when de' festival breaks. Dat' will be our signal to get back." I said.

"Okay, got it," Linc gave me a thumbs up.

Deddy stopped his horse and jumped down. He looked at me, walked to the door of the schoolhouse, and began working.

Bam, Linc, and I looked at each other but didn't say a word. We walked off silently; I pulled Hadie along towards the stable, Linc constantly looked over his shoulder; and Bam was nowhere in sight. In the back of my mind, I knew if Mamma found out or caught me, our relationship would be strained, forever. But that didn't stop me.

◆ ◆ ◆

Deddy finished the door and rode back home. He walked into the house but not before pulling his looking tube from his pocket and staring deep off into the water. Deddy eyed Meema and Mamma, while they were wrapping up their sewing.

"They's up to somethin'," Deddy informed Mamma.

"Who is up to something?" Mamma questioned.

"That chile of yours and her crew," Deddy responded.

Mamma eyed Meema then walked over to the sink to wash her hands.

"What makes you say that?" Mamma asked.

"Well, when I was leaving, the crew didn't say nuthin' to each other. They jus' looked very hard at each other and walked off, except Bam, she sprinted down the way. They don't normally do that. They always end with a joke or some thang' they do. That wasn't normal." Deddy turned his back.

"Maybe Baybruh, you just might be thankin' too hard about it." Mamma walked to the looking hole.

"May...Be! But I got my eye on'em."

Deddy disappeared behind his bedroom door.

The way Slope was set up kept everyone close. The schoolhouse sat dead smack in the middle of a circle at the end of a row of houses. Lilly, Gene, Paul, and Micha lived in the middle of Bam and me, which stretched seven houses down the row on our side of the strip. I lived in the house closest to the schoolhouse, opposite Pat but farthest from the big wooden gate with the bright red sign on it.

On the other side of the strip was a row of houses that were connected by a single rooftop. I was told that from the rooftop, you could see all of Slope. The men of Slope would spend hours up there meeting, drinking, and smoking pipes.

Every now and again, Meema would be asked to join them. I begged her to let me go, too.

"No," she would say sternly. "You know everyone is not allowed up top."

I was hardheaded and her words just made me want to go even more.

Mr. Stone, the wood maker, had the only house tucked off to the side, cottage-style that he built himself. It was a big beautiful home, as were most things that he made. He used to have two sons, Rok and Brik. Meema told me that Rok drowned when he was just learning to walk.

The way the story goes, his Momma had taken him and her new baby, Brik, down to the lake's edge to wash the linens. Rok, the oldest of the two got away from his Momma's watchful eye and walked right out into the lake. He was under for quite a while before she could get to him. Meema said he was so small that it took her a while to find him. When she finally did, they said his stomach was the size of a melon. Meema hated telling that story.

Some say his momma died from grief and because Brik was so young, he never knew who she was. She had to be a woman of a lighter tone because Brik had silky hair and lighter skin, too. Meema said skin tone doesn't matter too much when *we* have babies because they pop out in all different shades. It didn't matter too much to me because I never wanted anything popping out of me.

Meema went on to say, ever since that happened, Mr. Stone lost himself in his work. The women of Slope would say that they knew that he didn't want to marry again by the way that he kept himself. Meema always said that there ain't nobody that was born to live alone, no matter how bad they smell.

He smelled bad. I mean…really bad. Bad like old onions left in the sun. The women folk would joke that his stench was so strong that you could smell him before he got there. Despite all of that, everyone in Slope had what we needed and a little bit of what we wanted. Life was good.

CHAPTER 5

Unexpected Guests

The night before the festival felt like the calm before a storm, except everyone was too busy to notice. Nearly the entire village had gathered in the mess hall, voices rising in laughter and chatter, while elders and mothers with newborns stayed behind in their homes. The hall buzzed with the energy of preparation, and as always, we took our usual spots at the horseshoe-shaped table, with the younger children seated off to the side.

Suddenly, the doors burst open. Mr. Stone entered with urgency etched into his face, his boots echoing across the wooden floor. He walked directly to

Mamma and Deddy, leaning in close to whisper. The conversation that unfolded between them wasn't meant for anyone else. My eyes, however, couldn't help but circle the room, eventually locking with Bam and Linc's. Their expressions mirrored the growing tension I felt. We were all thinking the same thing; something was happening, and it wasn't good.

I refocused on the trio; Mamma, Deddy, and Mr. Stone. I began to eye their lips very closely until I heard their voices in my head.

"We gots' trouble," Mr. Stone whispered.

Deddy moved in closer.

I looked at Bam and she looked back at me. Linc was still staring at all three of them.

"Ship coming. Be here before dark," Mr. Stone muttered.

"How did it get so close unnoticed?" Deddy's voice was sharper now.

"Old Man Eddie fell asleep on lookout," Mr. Stone replied grimly.

Mamma, who'd been silent until now, crossed her arms.

"Baybruh. We gotta get rid of our problem right nah. We can't wait for tomorrow," Mamma said.

Deddy didn't hesitate. He stood abruptly, whispering something to Meema before disappearing out the door with Mamma and Mr. Stone. Meema rose next, her voice slicing through the room as she started singing. Her voice was like honey over jagged rocks, smoothing over the unease in the air.

One by one, the hall followed her lead, swaying and clapping along to the rhythm. The celebration became a perfect distraction. I lost Bam and Linc in it. I stumbled through the crowd for a while until I stepped on Linc's shoe.

"Damn, Bri. Your eyes open?" Linc complained.

"Where is Bam?" I asked.

"I found her and told her to stay over by de' door," Linc added.

"You seen my Mamma and Deddy?" the questions continued.

"Dey disappeared out of de' door, soon as your Meema started singing," Linc responded.

"Let's go get Bam," I demanded.

We walked over to the door and saw that Bam was peeking out of it very inconspicuously. I looked around to see if anyone was watching then I tapped her on the shoulder.

"Wait a minute. Som'ns goin' on," Bam whispered without turning around.

She turned to us, her face serious.

"Somethin's happenin', Yo' Mamma, Deddy, and Mr. Stone headed up toward the schoolhouse, armed to de' teeth and wearin' cloaks to blend in de' dark."

"Dat's just it?" I whispered.

"Yeah, and de' way dey moved, they don't want nobody knowin' what they doin'," Bam added.

Curiosity won over caution. We crept out the back of the mess hall, skirting shadows until we had a clear view of the schoolhouse trail. The hill sloped steeply into the riverbed, the quiet waters shimmering under the thin moonlight. Slope stood watch as always, silent yet powerful.

I knew exactly what Bam was talking about, but I didn't say anything. We all looked toward the river. Meema told me a story about how Slope is a protector of its people, and the river is his right hand. She warns him of danger and he protects her from it.

Sometimes the river splashes into Slope as if they are in a lover's quarrel. When this happens, Slope pushes the water back out to sea, but the river never loses her will. She always comes back and sometimes with vengeance. But on occasion, the river and Slope are really sweet on each other; especially at the end of a storm when the river is no longer angry. And instead of smacking, she softly kisses Slope's edge and in return, he gently sends chills down her spine that ripple and sparkle in the moonlight.

Then came the sound of hoofbeats. A masked rider bolted past the hall, carrying a cotton sack slung low on the back of his horse. From out of the sack, stretched a hand dripping with blood.

My stomach lurched. Our mouths dropped. I started pacing.

All I could think about was the secrets that Meema spoke of and about the masked riders who raided ships.

"Shhh! Here come some mo'. And dey all have sacks on de' back of'em." Linc said quietly.

"What in the…" Bam breathed, unable to finish her sentence.

We ducked back behind the mess hall, one on top of the other to get a better look. One last horse pulled up to the mess hall. It was Mr. Stone. He jumped off his nag, wiped the sweat and blood from his hands with his hat, then stuffed his hat in his pants and walked into the mess hall as if nothing happened.

Bam, Linc, and I slid in behind him, pretending we'd been there all along. We walked off in separate ways with our eyes locked on him.

Mr. Stone found Meema in the midst of the celebration. They began to talk. In the middle of the conversation, Meema tried to mask her alarm, but I caught the slight recoil in her stance. Meema looked Mr. Stone in the eye with awe for a quick instant, and then she covered her nose.

They continued to whisper and then with a piercing whistle, Meema signaled the end of the gathering. Everyone trickled through the doors and out into the open. I found Bam, Linc, Gene, and Paul right outside of the door.

"Are we still on for tomorrow?" Bam asked.

We all started walking in the direction of our row. Jholie runs up behind us unnoticed. I turned then whistled. The crew huddled back up with Jholie, now seen, off to the side.

"What's going on tomorrow?" Gene questioned. We all looked at Gene.

"After our show, meet at de' edge of de' fence closest to de' woods. Stay on your horses so dat dey don't spec' nu'in'. Remember to bring what I told you to bring," I reiterated.

"Okay," Bam confirmed. Linc and Paul nodded. Gene looked confused.

"OH! De' plan?" Gene finally caught on. "Wait, what supplies?" Gene asked,

Paul smacked Gene on the back of the neck. The two horse-played until they heard my voice.

"Everything we need to figure out what's really goin' on," I said, glaring at him. "And one last word, don't say nu'in' to nobody. If we gon' do dis we gotta keep dis 'tween us. See y'all when de' sun come up," I pointed at Gene and Paul.

Gene nodded reluctantly. Bam and Paul exchanged knowing looks.

"And remember," I added, my voice dropping to a fierce whisper. "Not a word to anyone. This stays 'tween us."

The crew scattered quietly, each slipping into the dark like shadows, carrying the weight of the unspoken. Something big was unfolding, and come tomorrow, we'd be in the thick of it.

♦ ♦ ♦

Deddy coiled a heavy chain tightly around the latch of the weathered gate nearest to the river. The night air was thick, heavy with silence, but for the restless snort of Ham, his faithful horse, standing guard not far off.

The sound wasn't random, Ham's instincts were sharp, and Deddy had trained him well. Someone was coming. Deddy's hand froze mid-wipe as he glanced up. The bloodied rag in his hand felt heavier now. From the shadows emerged Mamma, her stride purposeful, her form cloaked in dark clothing, and his hat perched jauntily on her head. Beside her walked a man Deddy didn't recognize. The newcomer's face was hard as stone, his stance confident.

"Baybruh," Mamma began as they came closer, "this here is Smalls from the ship. He ain't planning to stay long, just a couple of days. Says he'll help us with our... problem, seeings that we helped him."

Deddy studied the man. "You sho' you

can handle it, Mr. Smalls?" The newcomer
stepped forward, unfazed.

"Call me Bobby," he said, voice
gravelly with conviction. "And yeah, I
can handle it. Been time they knew how
it feels to be hunted."

Baybruh nodded slowly.

"Aight, Baybruh. But we still don't
know who fathered that child," he added,
his voice dipping low with caution.

"Could throw the whole plan outta
whack," Deddy said.

Mamma shot a glance toward Bobby.

"This stays between us. Understood?"

Bobby smirked. "Ain't nothin' leaves
my lips without my say-so." His
expression darkened. "But y'all best keep
watch. Word is Injuns been seen nearby,
and they ain't takin' kindly to
settlers."

Mamma looked at Mr. Smalls from head
to toe. "Settlers? I ain't no settla'."
Mamma looked at him hard. "We gotta get
back and get some rest. Festival in the
mornin'," Mamma added without a blink.

They all mount their horses.

"Smalls you can stay the night with us if you like, we gots'a extra bed," Deddy offered.

"Call me Bobby. No, thanks, Suh. I'll be sleeping on my ship with the rest of my crew. Don't forget, Injuns travelin' roun'. They might be close, so y'all need to be 'ware." Mr. Smalls walked off.

As they spoke, the river whispered in the distance, its murmurs curling up the slope like an eavesdropper. Baybruh leaned closer to Bobby.

"How'd a man like you end up with a ship anyhow?"

You ever been a slave, Suh?" Mr. Smalls questioned.

"No, I was bone' here but I have heard a tale or two," Baybruh said.

"I thought so. Well, you don' know what it's like and I's ain't got time to 'xplain it.

Deddy offers, "Mr. Smalls, I got some shine' and a cigar if you want to sit a spell."

Mr. Smalls turned and looked at

Deddy. "Call me Bobby." Bobby's eyes glittered with something between rage and pride.

"Long story short? I was born a slave, Suh. My Massa, not my Paw. Unlike most, I was told that my Mistress was my real Maw, and the only truth to it was we had the same kind of eyes." Bobby paused.

Baybruh's mouth hung opened with awe.

"Anyway, this skin allowed me to work right next to the Massa and with that came trus'. One night, drunk as a fish, he left me and my crew on his ship while he stumbled off to mourn his Misses, my Mamma I'se suppose. The way the story go, Injuns took her, but my kin say she wanted to go." Bobby's voice dropped, now laced with venom. "He beat on us, y'see, for the pain he couldn't drown in spirits."

He paused, his grip tightening on the reins. "That night, I saw my chance. Slipped that ship right outta the harbor, found my wife and a few others on the way out. Been on the sea ever since, but I keep my ear to the ground. Heard them Injuns got bones to pick, and they out there, somewhere close. I been on the sea for about seb'm, eight years nah'."

"How you know so much about Injuns," Mamma sassed. "I bet you wouldn't know one if you seen one?"

"I seen plenty, Mam," Mr. Smalls snaps back with a lie. "But I ain't scared."

"You and your crew come to the festival tomorrow," Deddy interrupted, eager now. "We got plenty of food, and seats right up front. Y'all can be our special gues'. I can't wait to meet'em." Deddy said eagerly.

"Much obliged, Mam and Suh." Mr. Smalls was pleased.

When Bobby turned to leave, the dark closed in behind him. Deddy and Mamma mounted their horses and headed back to the barn. They dismounted quietly, opening the barn doors to the sharp scent of hay...and something else.

"Smells like Stoney been here," Mamma quipped, but her smile faded as their lantern's glow revealed Mr. Stone, slumped in a corner of the barn, his head in his hands.

"Stoney?" Deddy's voice was tight.

"What are you doin' here?"

Stoney looked up, shame etched into his face. "There's somethin' y'all need to know... 'Bout the problem under the schoolhouse."

"What is it, Stoney?" Mamma questioned.

"That problem we got under the schoolhouse…" Stoney said.

Deddy cut him off. "Ain't nothin' to know, Stoney. We'll deal with it. Then things go back to normal."

But Stoney's face twisted with doubt. "Baybruh... you sure 'bout that?" he murmured, moving toward the door.

"Wait, what you have to tell us?" Mamma said quickly.

"Don't matter no mo." Before either of them could stop him, Stoney disappeared into the night.

Deddy and Mamma walked the horses to their stables. They walked to the corner of the barn where Deddy kept his hats next to three hooks hanging from a 4x4 nailed to the barn wall. Two hooks held Deddy's hat and a third held Mamma's housedress.

Deddy shut the barn door with a sigh, but Mamma touched his arm, grounding him in the moment. He turned to see her peel away the dark clothing, tossing them aside. She reached for her dress, but Deddy. caught her wrist, his gaze locking hers.

"You ain't needin' that just yet," he whispered, his voice thick with longing.

"I see what you are thinking," Mamma whispered. "You must be thinking it too," Deddy responded.

"Well, you could never resist." Mamma slowly kissed his chest.

"Never." Deddy passionately sighed then rubbed her hair.

Deddy laid Mamma on the hay, then gently laid on top of her. He kissed her forehead and breast. She easily becomes enchanted by his gentleness and lets him have his way for a moment. Then she aggressively flipped him over so that he is on the bottom and she is now on top. In the quiet of the barn, under the protective cover of darkness, they let the world and its troubles fade, if only for a moment. Their whispered breaths and tender movements drowned out the weight of the secrets they kept and the storm creeping ever closer.

When they were done, they dressed in silence, their bond unspoken but unbreakable. As they walked toward the house hand-in-hand, neither spoke of what awaited them at the festival, or beyond it. Some truths were too heavy to bear even in the darkness of the night.

CHAPTER 6

The Festival

The morning of the festival brought an unsettling chill, the kind that crept up your sleeves and clung to your skin. The wind howled through the bending trees and rippling cornstalks, a restless force that couldn't be ignored. Even the earth seemed unwilling to cooperate; the softened walkways squelched beneath boots, unsuitable for riding. Above, the sun teased the clouds in a relentless game of hide-and-seek, finally emerging victorious in a blaze of gold.

Despite the crisp air, excitement coursed through Slope like an unseen current, its energy as palpable as the wind itself. I climbed out of bed that morning with a restless readiness, not just for the festival, but for the plan we had been hatching. I dressed quickly, tugging on my costume with trembling hands, then waited at the front of the house for Bam and Linc. They were late. When they arrived, their breaths were ragged, their faces flushed as if they'd run the whole way.

"Hey, Bri," Bam panted. "Sorry we're late. Old Mr. Stone showed up at the house last night, jawing with my daddy 'til near dawn. Ain't been a wink of sleep for me."

"She ain't lying," Linc added with a laugh. "Took forever to wake her, too. Bet she didn't even wash her—"

"Shut up Linc. I did wash. Anyway, y'all ready?" Bam got serious.

"Yeah, I am ready but more for de' plan dan' de' festival. Did y'all bring de stuff?" I questioned.

Linc held up a brown sack, "Got it. Let's head to the stable and get dressed there."

I threw their uniforms at them. They caught them simultaneously, almost as if

it was part of our act. I swung up onto
Hadie, and we made our way to the stables.
But as we approached the stable doors, a
sound stopped us; a muffled cry. It was
coming from the outhouse. Linc crept
forward, easing the door open.

Inside, Mr. Stone sat hunched over,
sobbing so hard his body shook. The air
inside was rank, an acrid stench that made
my stomach churn. The stench clung to him,
a grim specter, just as Meema said.

I walked over to him and tried to
place my hand on his back but the air
stank so bad that I decided against it.
Mr. Stone was just as shocked as we were.
He stepped raggedly out from the outhouse
to grab the door, and I knew at that
moment, the outhouse alone didn't smell
that bad.

"Gon' bout yo' biness'," Mr. Stone
growled, his voice ragged as he slammed
the door behind him. We walked away from
Mr. Stone facing backward. We didn't take
our eyes off him except to look at Linc.
We stepped back slowly, each of us
shooting glances at Linc. We knew he was

dying to make some joke about the scene.

"Well, Linc? Let's hear it," I
prompted.

"Hear what?" Linc asked innocently.
Bam crossed her arms.

"C'mon, we know you got somethin' to
say."

But Linc just shrugged. "Ain't got
nothin'. I feel bad for him, honestly."

Bam and I exchanged wide-eyed looks,
caught off guard by his unexpected
restraint. For a moment, we saw something
new in him, something grown-up. But just
as quickly, we shoved it aside and
trudged toward the meadow.

The festival meadow sat just beyond
the woods behind the schoolhouse. The
quickest route was through the trees, and
once we emerged, it was as if the world
transformed. The meadow was a riot of
color, Sara's flowers blooming in every
corner. She was the only one who could
coax such beauty from the earth, and
she'd outdone herself this year. Vibrant
bouquets dotted the village, hidden
surprises that whispered her love for the

festival. The distance from the stables to the meadow was a nice ride but it was worth it. She loved the festival just as much as Mamma.

The ride to the stables was quiet, punctuated only by the crunch of leaves underfoot. We finally made it to the stables. Bam and Linc got dressed behind the barn doors. I waited. And waited…And waited till I crept behind the barn doors and found those two lip-locked together. I wasn't in shock as much as I pretended.

"Ooh!" I exclaimed, smirking. "I knew it!"

"Knew what?" Bam snapped, face turning crimson.

"You two are sweet on each other!" Linc looked at Bam, both of them still half-naked.

"You might as well show her!" Linc blurted out.

"Show me what?" I questioned.

Linc glanced nervously at Bam, who hesitated for only a moment before lifting the top of her costume. Beneath it, a subtle bulge curved her stomach. My breath caught as the realization hit me.

"You're... pregnant?" I whispered, stunned.

Bam nodded, her lips tightening. I pulled her into a hug, then hugged Linc for good measure. But practical thoughts pushed their way into my mind.

"Bam, you can't ride today. And you definitely can't run in the annual race!"

"What do you mean I can't ride and I can't run?" Bam snapped back.

"You can't. What if you fall off or fall down?" I pointed at her belly.

Bam put her hands on her hips.

"Don't be trying to tell me what to do, Bri. You ain't my Momma."

"She's right you know, Bam." Linc interrupted.

"SHUT UP, Linc!" we yelled in unison.

"We don't need your help.

"Shhh! You hear dat?" Linc walked to the door. A sharp sound outside silenced us.

Footsteps.

"Someone's coming. Hurry up get dressed, but dis' ain't over." I whispered.

"Promise, you won't tell a soul, Bri," Bam looked concerned.

"I promise, girl," I assured Bam.

Not just for her, but for my sake, too.

Deddy swung the barn door open while holding Ham by the saddle. Next to him stood a man I've never seen before. He wore funny clothes like the men Meema spoke about who she once saw aboard a ship. He wasn't a tall man. He looked stubby.

"Youngins, this here is Mr. Smalls. He's on a short trip, just passing through. He'll be staying for the festival and sail out soon after." Deddy stepped to the side.

We weren't used to folks just passing through, that's cause most folks stayed and made Slope their home. I walked up to the stubby man and spoke. Deddy tried to introduce me, but I had my own way of introducing myself.

The man tipped his hat, his gaze scanning us. I stepped forward, already determined to do things my way.

"Welcome. I hope you enjoy your time in Slope. How did you…" I started to say.

"This fast-talking gal is my oldest chile, Bri. She's just 'bout fifteen," Deddy said, cutting into the conversation. "And these here are her best friend, Bam, and her cousin, Linc."

"How do you do, Suh?" Bam greeted politely, nodding her head.

"Welcome," Linc added, sticking out his hand for a quick shake. Mr. Smalls accepted it but barely held on for a second before letting go.

"Well, folks are starting to gather. Y'all ready, right? Yo' show is the gran' finale," Deddy said while he wrapped Ham's neck rope around a pole.

"What Deddy? I thought we were going first?" I said.

"Nope, we had to move some things around to 'commodate our gues'," Deddy replied.

"Yeah we heading out, now," Bam said quickly while she dragged Linc and me toward the stables in the back.

We worked quickly, saddling our horses in silence. Linc tossed me the sack with the stuff, Bam did the same. I hung the sacks on Deddy's hat hook tucked under two hats.

"We will ride back round' and grab'em after our show," I added.

We barely had time to breathe before the sound of Deddy's voice and Mr. Smalls' footsteps outside sent us scrambling.

Slipping out the back, we led our horses to the meadow, walking instead of riding to keep their energy fresh.

I couldn't stop thinking about what Linc and Bam had done in making a baby and how our lives would change forever.

Although I was happy for them, it made me wonder about what would be expected of me. When everyone found out, would they look to me for the next baby? I hated Bam and Linc for that, I wanted no parts of it and there they go, inserting me in it.

I had a bad feeling about Bam riding and running in the race but I didn't say nothing, I kept it to myself. It reminded me of the tales Meema used to tell me 'bout how I was riding before I was born. She said Mamma was of the stubborn type and didn't listen to a warning from no one. She rode her horse so much they thought that I'd be born on one.

We finally reached the meadow. There were tents set up all over the place. Mr. Burns had a tent for his birds. Miss Jade had pools for her fish. There were two face-painting tents for the little kids that Lilly and Pat worked out of. The activities went on and on from puppet shows, horseshoes, sack races, and plenty of food.

The main show took place in the center of two rows that were neatly decorated by Sara. This was where Bam, Linc, and I were going to perform. This is also where the annual race was held.

The festival always started with the sounding of the drums. Gene and Paul were the best drummers in Slope and it was their job to set the tone. After Gene and Paul signaled the start of the festival, the elders would lead us in praise, followed by a poem from Brik, the hugging ceremony, the dance, then the annual race and the final show.

CHAPTER 7

Unforeseen

Brik is Mr. Stone's only son, he be bout' my age. Most of the time he helps his dad with wood-making. Other than that, you'll find him standing alone having what may look like a conversation with himself, but we all know he's just reciting poetry. It's funny to watch. Sometimes he gets so into that he forgets that he is outside around other people. You can tell he loved it. Brik is the top student in our class and spends the rest of his free time at the school, writing or helping Miss Jones.

When the elders are ready, we make a big circle, hold hands, and wait for Old Man Eddie to start the prayer.

"Let's give thanks to the most-high. May we continue to be blessed for the rest

of our days," Old Man Eddie said with a
raspy voice while holding his arms in the
air.

"Yes'm," voices from the crowd.

By this time, everyone who is
attending, has found their way to the
meadow. Brik, Mr. Stone's only son, steps
into the center of the circle dressed in
black, spun dramatically, and bowed.

"I call this one, Ballad of a
Bastard," Brik yelled.

"OOH; AHH," from voices in the crowd
followed by finger snaps.

"You took my Momma
And stole her right to say no.
You beat my Momma,
Left scars the world will never know.
You raped my Momma,
Claimed power with no remorse.
You took my Momma,
Yet I stand, your shameful source.
You beat my Momma,
But her strength flows in my veins.
You raped my Momma,
Now I rise, breaking your chains."
You took my Momma

Blessed by a bastardly lamb

You beat my Momma

Black and blue with swollen hands

You raped my Momma

Now you don't know WHO or WHERE I AM!"

Finger *SNAP, SNAP, SNAPS* filled the air. The drums sounded once again. The people of Slope start the hugging ceremony. It's not really called the hugging ceremony. I just call it that because that is what this part looks like, but there was a catch to it. Whomever you were hugging when the drums went off was your dance partner.

I ducked and dodged through the crowd hoping that no one was eyeing me but low and behold, Brik made sure I was in his grasp when the drums went BOOM! It felt like Gene and Paul were watching me the entire time, or Brik set this up. Gene and Paul started banging on their drums as soon as he was next to me. Bam just so happened to be partnered with Linc. That wasn't by chance, either.

When the song was just about over,

Brik tried to kiss me on the cheek. He leaned in on my right, I dipped back on my left. He leaned in on my left, so I dipped back on my right. He finally figured out that I didn't want to be kissed and backed off.

Old Man Eddie blew his whistle to start the annual race. It was Linc, Bam, Gene, Paul, Brik, and me in our age category. We all lined up at the edge of the path. I looked at Bam and she knew why. On the other hand, she had a different look in her eye. Victory.

I ran, just for fun, but Bam ran for glory. Gene, Paul, Linc, and Brik ran for bragging rights. In the end, Bam always came out on top. I mean every year since she started running in the race she was always the winner.

"Fool, you wish you could beat me," Linc tells Paul.

"Bruh, you ain't gonna be sayin' nu'in' with all dis' dust in yo' mouth," Paul responded.

"I'on't' know why you talkin' to him. I wore my favorite britches so y'all

can enjoy de' view from my backside,"
joked Gene as he tugged on his britches.

"This ain't no fancy show, and
anyway, ain't nobody lookin' at yo'
backside besides crazy Sara," Brik added.

"But for me on the other hand…" Brik
looked over his shoulder to see some of
the other girls gawking at him.

"I'm only running to be next to one."
Brik looked at me.

I gather every drop of fluid in my
mouth and spat it out hard on the ground.
Brik started grinning while his fan club
acted disgusted. Old Man Eddie blew his
warning blow. We quickly lined back up.

The whistle blew and we all took off,
Bam in the lead. Gene, Paul, Linc, and I
were right on her tail. Gene eased out in
front of us all. Then Paul. Then Linc.
Then me. Brik was nowhere in sight. And
before you know it, we all had passed Bam.
I lost track of the race and looked back
at her. She was running hard but it wasn't
her hardest. I could tell, but the guys
didn't even notice. Gene looked over at
Paul and Linc with a devilish grin.

"Like my britches," Gene panted and took off like lightning.

Gene came in first, Linc in second, Paul in third, me in fourth, Bam in fifth, and Brik dead last. By the time we made it to the finish line, the younger kids were already lined up, waiting their turn. When their race was over, Micah and Gene received a wooden medal made by Mr. Stone who promised to engrave and polish it up real nice. Bam was pissed and stormed off. I followed right behind her.

Bam, hold up!" I called, catching up.

"I could've won," she muttered, her face hard, but her eyes gave her away.

"No, you couldna. And you know why." I got nose-to-nose with Bam.

"Watch it Bri." Bam put her hands on her hips.

"I didn't tell you to do what you done," I turned away.

"What you mean by dat?" Bam questioned.

"You went and made a baby. What was you spectin', Bam? Everything to stay the same?" I turned back to Bam.

Bam looked at me sideways.

"Well, you know what I mean. We suppose to ride around de' world. How we gone do dat wi' a baby. You just don't know what you've done." I turned my back.

She glared at me, then sighed, letting some of the fire drain from her voice.

"What did I do Bri? Girls have babies all of de' time." Bam reasoned.

I walked right up to Bam, face-to-face again, "WHAT ABOUT US, WHAT ABOUT ME?!"

"Bri, do you hear yo'self, right now? Dat's selfish as hell," Bam looked disappointed.

"Once dis' gets out you gonna have Mamma, Deddy, and all of Slope lookin' at me. Like I'm next," I said angrily.

"Bri, I'm having a baby. I'm not changing your world. And do you know how bad dat' shit hurts? I heard some girls don't make it." Bam looked worried.

Her words hit me like a gut punch, cutting through my anger. I never thought about the things that Bam was saying. My

life without Bam, never. I started to feel
like shit, real quick, but something in me
still felt like I was being left behind
and put on the spot all at the same time.

"My bad, Bam," I hugged her tight.

"I'm scared Bri." Bam hugged me back.

"I got your back, pickaninny. But
promise me, no more stunts after today."

I pointed my finger at the tip of her
nose.

Bam nodded, but her face still held a
weight I couldn't ignore. "Okay. Once my
Mamma finds out, it's all over anyway."

"What? She didn't tell you. I already
told her," I joked.

Bam slapped the back of my neck. We
walked back toward the festival together,
something unspoken passing between us. It
felt weird yet comforting. Whatever came
next, we'd face it together. For now, the
sound of drums and laughter wrapped us in
the warmth of Slope, and we let ourselves
disappear into it. The drums sounded once
again and the people of Slope poured out
into the meadow.

Jholie was first in line for face

painting; she loved rainbows like they were a piece of her. Lilly had a gift with the brush that made magic come to life, and though Pat was still finding her way, she was miles ahead of most.

The festival was a tapestry of joy, with brown faces glowing in the warm light of community. Even Mr. Smalls, a man not easily impressed, seemed taken in by the scene. I caught a snippet of his conversation with Deddy as I wandered past the overflowing food tables.

"Baybruh, dis' right here? This a mighty fine gathering y'all gots'," Mr. Smalls said, biting deeply into a grilled turkey leg. His wife and kids hovered nearby, waiting to claim their share.

Bam crept up behind me.

"Don't dey' know dey' can each have one, why are dey' sharing," whispered Bam.

"Everybody ain't eating for two and you're already starting to show," I whispered back to Bam. Bam put her whole hand over my mouth and shook my head back and forth.

"SHHH, you promised." Bam finally

freed me from her grasp.

"Alright." I got serious and snatched her hand off my face.

"The main event is about to begin, let's find Linc and get de' horses." Bam walked away.

"Mr. Smalls." Deddy stood on his feet. "Once my show is done, we can go handle that problem. And please tell your crew to eat up, no need to share food, we have plenty," Deddy pointed to the food tables.

Mr. Smalls turned and looked at his crew, then smiled.

"Well, you heard what the man said, dig in."

The spread was a feast for the eyes and the soul. The table had the best of everything on it; gumbo, chicken, fish, greens, bananas, grapes, apples, peaches, every pie you can think of, cakes, turkey legs, macaroni, and shrimp to name a few. It even had some traditional foods from the Meema's first home, like Fufu, plantains, couscous, and Jollof rice.

Our guests were overwhelmed. They

didn't know where to begin. They did what
any hungry belly would do, get a little
bit of everything. After their plates were
full, Deddy guided them to a good spot to
watch the main event. They were seated
with plates in hand.

Deddy disappeared into the woods.

Soon, drums rolled like thunder. Gene
and Paul signaled the start of the main
event. Deddy emerged from the trees,
mounted on his prized stallions, their
coats shimmering under the fading sun.

Gene and Paul worked with Deddy on
training the steeds to recognize the drum
sounds. Deddy worked wonders with those
beasts. They moved with grace to the beat,
bowing, stepping backward, and waving to
the crowd as if they'd rehearsed it all
their lives.

The audience gasped and clapped as
Deddy and his horses melted back into the
woods. Deddy and his stallions disappeared
in the woods. Drums sounded once again.

Out came the dancers.

The drums came alive again,
announcing the dancers. They took the

stage, swaying and leaping in unison, followed by Jholie and Sam's captivating mime routine. Next was Sara's flower fashion show. She used the little kids for display. They walked out in uneven lines stomping down the walkway. Their Mommas and Daddies gleamed with pride as they walked past. This was where we usually missed the fun—it was time to prep for our act. But where was Deddy? He never missed Sara's part.

When the aisle cleared, we emerged, standing tall on our horses. Bam led the way, and the crowd roared as we formed a triangle. We dropped into the saddles and thundered toward one another, rearing our horses back in perfect symmetry. The cheers grew louder. Although this sounded easy, it was difficult to pull off. I would jump on Bam's horse, Linc on mine, and Bam on Linc's horse. It was even scarier knowing about Bam's condition.

It was time. Linc's gaze lingered on me, full of unspoken worry, but there was no turning back now. I knew that it was not from his nervousness. He was worried

about Bam and truth be told, I was too. I
mean, I was pissed about what they had
done but she was my best friend and he was
my favorite cousin. Nonetheless, we pulled
it off with perfection then rode hard to
the stables. They clapped and hollered,
their voices chasing us as we disappeared
into the distance, hearts pounding and
legs aching, but the plan was set in
motion.

CHAPTER 8

The Door in the Floor

As I rode toward the stables to grab the supplies, I caught sight of Bam just ahead. I passed Bam, a rare moment of being the first to arrive. I sprinted into the barn, heading straight for the spot where I'd stashed the sacks. But when I got there, my heart sank, they were gone.

"The stuff's not here!" I yelled, my voice sharp with panic.

Linc and Bam were right behind me, leaping off their horses and rushing inside.

"Are you sure this is the right spot?" Linc asked, glancing around as if the bags might magically appear.

"Of course, I'm sure!" I snapped, grabbing hold of the empty hook where the sacks should have been hanging. "This is exactly where I put it!"

Bam's expression darkened, her jaw tightening as realization struck.

"Somebody knows about our plan," she muttered, her words laced with anger.

"No way, even if dey' got de' sacs, dey' don't know what de' stuff is for," I added.

"What do we do for protection? I'on't reckon dis' is a good idea no mo'." Linc said hesitantly, his worry obvious.

"Please, Linc. Don't back out now," I beseeched him. "We can do this. We *have* to do this. We don't have much time," I pleaded.

Without waiting for a response, I jumped onto Hadie and rode off into the woods, my heart pounding. Bam and Linc lagged behind, taking their time.

"Well, we can't let her go by herself," Bam said.

"I know. Let's go." Linc kicked his horse and took off.

They caught up to me near the schoolhouse, and we slowed as we reached the fence. I was relieved.

"I see yo' Deddy wasn't playing wi' dat chain," Linc muttered, eyeing the heavy lock and sturdy links.

"I already knew, dat' de' gate nor de' schoolhouse door wasn't an option. De' only way I see it, we gotta go over Mr. Stone's fence. Dere' are nails on de' tops of de boards. When we step we gotta make sure we stand den' skip one board," I demonstrated, picking one foot up at a time.

"Linc, since you're de tallest, stand on Jack to see what's on de' other side. We don't need any extra stunts by Mr. Stone," Bam suggested.

Linc mounted his horse, Jack. He was the only one of us tall enough to stand and look over to the other side with ease.

"It's just a yard but it's divided."

He pointed to an area behind the fence.

"What do you mean?" I questioned.

"You know how dere' is a yard behind de' schoolhouse, de' one we hang in?" Linc pointed over the fence.

"Yeah," I agreed.

"Well dere' is another one behind dat' one. It's fenced in. It has a raggedy barn sittin' in de' middle of it." Linc made a circle with his hands.

"I always wondered why dat' fence sat so high. We gotta get in dat barn," I started to pace back and forth.

Without hesitation, Linc climbed the fence and jumped over. Bam went next and then me. We landed quietly and safe, but a sharp, piercing cry startled us. It was a baby. Our eyes met, wide with alarm, and then darted toward the barn. Creeping forward, we reached the door. Linc opened it, and a foul stench hit us so hard I gagged.

"Damn, Bri, you break wind or somethin'?" Linc teased.

"Smells more like Mr. Stone," Bam cracked as we shared a brief laugh, but then we got serious because the smell was recognizable. The smell was unmistakable and disturbing. It reminded me of Sara's old basket of sanitary cloths left too long in the meadow, as she tried to mask the stench with flowers.

My stomach churned. This woman, actually thought, the smell of flowers would supersede dried blood. We went looking for the source of the stench.

"I heard it more from undernea' dis pile of hay." Linc walked over to the source of the stench. Linc said, stepping forward. He kicked at the hay, uncovering a heavy wooden door in the floor.

"It came from undernea' dat' doe' in de' floor."

"Wow! Linc for noticing," I said sarcastically.

Now things were getting weirder by the minute. Not only did the barn have a door on the floor with a key lock on it, but the key was still in the lock and it glowed in the dark.

"Why would someone lock something but leave the key?" I asked, leaning down.

Bam and Linc looked confused.

"No idea, but it looks fresh," Bam added nervously as I turned the glowing key. The lock snapped open with an eerie click. Linc reached down and heaved the door upward, revealing a staircase leading into darkness. The smell was even worse coming from below.

"Peeeuuuww. Dat's definitely Mr. Stone's smell and it's coming from down dere'." Bam leaned over and grabbed her stomach. The snack she had at the festival decorated the barn floor and added an even fouler smell to the barn, but we didn't let that turn us around.

"Dis' must lead to de' basement of de' schoolhouse," Linc looked in. "I'm going in."

Linc slowly crept down the steps with Bam close behind. They reached the bottom. Linc's foot brushed up against something in the darkness. He felt around and came up on two lanterns with a box of matches set off to the side of the hole.

"It's fresh oil in bof' ov'em." Linc said as he picked up the lanterns and smelled them.

"Stop playin'," I yelled down the damp whole. "You hear dat'?" I questioned.

We all get quiet.

"Yeah it's dark as hell down dere', too Bri," Bam interrupted.

99

"You scared or som'n," I questioned again.

"No, but I ain't crazy neither," Linc said.

"Just get de' lantern, I'll go first."

I started to make my way down the steps.

Linc handed me the lantern and I lit it on the first try. I held the lantern up over my head to reveal a long pathway with sconces on the wall about a foot apart.

Linc took the second lantern and lit it but a strange wind whistled through the barn and blew out the flame.

"Shit," Linc said softly. "That was a sign."

"Let me try," Bam interjected. Bam took the lantern and lit it.

I waited.

"Ladies first," Linc beckoned Bam to go.

I walked down the hallway, a little way, while Linc and Bam stayed behind. It looked like there was a door at the end. A desperate scream suddenly echoed from ahead.

"AHHHHH!"

Followed by an ominous moan echoing down the tunnel sending chills down our spines. The sound made me freeze, my blood turning cold.

"We should head back," Bam's voice quivered with fear.

"Not yet," my curiosity was burning now.

The crying intensified as we approached the door. Faint knocks followed, then the muffled voice of someone begging.

"Ge…Get me out of here!"

Linc moved to unchain the door, but Bam grabbed his arm.

"Wait. We don't know who, or *what*, is behind that door."

"There's a baby, Bam. We can't just leave it," Linc felt concerned.

"But why is there a baby *and* a voice behind this door? None of this makes sense!" I reasoned.

As we argued, a crescendo of noises erupted, chains rattling, steps from above, banging on the door in the hallway.

The barn seemed to come alive with sound.

I passed both of them up as I headed back to the steps. Startled, I fell up several steps and dropped the lantern at the bottom, but it stayed lit. The screaming stopped.

Linc and Bam paused for a brief moment to share a kiss. Bam stepped slowly down the dark hallway, Linc followed closely behind her. They made it to the first sconce. Linc held the lantern above his head and took Bam's hand. They walked down the path behind me.

"Ahhhhhhhhhhh!" a voice yelled from behind the door that froze us in our tracks but also sparked our curiosity.

Linc dropped the lantern and the screaming stopped. He picked up the lantern but the flame was out.

"Y'all hear dat," whispered Bam.

"No," I responded.

"I know, dat's de' problem," Bam replied.

The ominous moaning that once sent chills down our spines had ceased. I used my hand to beckon them up the ladder, but

Linc turned around with Bam on his heels.

Whatever or whoever is on the other side of this door knows that we are here. Linc giggled the handle without restraint from Bam. The door was locked from the outside. We could get in, but whatever was on the inside couldn't get out.

BANG BANG BANG!

Knocks echoed from behind the door.

Cries from a baby are heard, and then more knocks. I jumped with fear from above the whole.

"Get me out of here," a voice requested from behind the door.

Linc began to unravel the chain. Bam grabbed him and pulled him aside. She placed her ear to the door and listened.

"Wait. We don't know who dat' is," Bam said.

"All's I know, it sounds like dey' need help. It's a baby down here Bam," Linc reached for the door.

"But, why is it a voice and a baby behind dis' door?" Bam snapped back.

"Man dis' shits crazy!" I yelled to both of them.

Drums sound off in the distance.

"Dat's Gene and Paul!" I yelled again.

"We best get going," Bam suggested.

"We can't just leave'em," Linc pleaded.

"Oh de' hell we can," Bam argued.

"Will y'all two stop ya' bickering for a moment and let me figure dis out." I started to pace back and forth, again.

Footsteps are heard at the other end of the hall near the steps.

"Someone's coming," I hissed, turning towards the barn door.

We started walking slowly back to the steps. We heard a crescendo of sounds coming from every direction. First, a chain rattled on the barn door. Next, steps are heard from above and then BANG BANG BANG BANG is heard from behind the hallway door, again. Our pace picked up as we approached the barn doors. To our surprise and relief, Gene and Paul were standing on the other side.

"Hey, yo' Deddy, Mamma, and his guest are on deir' way here. I can hear your Deddy unraveling his chain on the fence."

104

Paul whispered quickly.

Bam and Linc hurried up the dark steps, Linc being last to ascend.

"Okay, let's go. Make sure we put dis' stuff back like we found it."

I walked to the door on the floor and began to close it.

"Bam where is de' lantern?" I questioned.

"It's all de' way back at de' door," Linc answered as we all looked at the door on the floor.

"Somebody's gotta go get it," Bam said as I slammed the door shut.

"To hell wi' de' light, let's go,"

Linc started for the barn door.

"No please, please, no no no," is heard from the hole in the ground.

"No time for it," I said.

A desperate cry rang out: "No, please! Don't leave me!"

"Who is dat?" Gene and Paul said simultaneously.

"Where is de' lock wi' de' key?" I questioned.

"I don't know; I can't find it," Linc

scurried around the barn.

By this time Gene and Paul were frantic. Linc had to smack Paul just to calm him down. Once Paul came to his senses, he couldn't speak. Gene got worried. Although they fought most of the time, they were like brothers. And the last thing that Gene wanted is for something to happen to Paul.

Gene walked up face to face with Paul and shook him so hard he had to speak.

"Okay, Okay, I'm okay," Paul panted.

You could see the relief on Gene's face.

CHAPTER 9

Blood on the Leaves

We all looked frantically around the raggedy, smelly barn for a moment. I picked up the lantern that still had a flame and searched around the barn. I stumbled on something hard covered. I brushed the hay away to find a wooden coffin. I held the lantern up high to reveal that there were several coffins covered in hay.

"Hey, hey, hey, LOOK!" I slowly moved away from the coffins.

"What Bri, we don't have time," Bam brushed me off but noticed that I was as stiff as rigor mortis. They all walked over to the back of the barn.

"Is dat' what I 'specs it is?" Paul

questioned.

"No no no no, dis can't be happening," Bam stuttered.

"What de' fuck is going on?" Linc grabbed his head.

Paul walked over to a coffin and uncovered more of the hay. He tried to raise the coffin slightly and something moved around inside then a spider crawled out drew back on his legs and sneered at Paul. Paul dropped the coffin.

"Glad it's nailed shut," Paul brushed away more hay.

"But look it's stacked on top of mo' coffins. Dese' coffins must be at least six high," Gene moved away.

We all looked at each other in awe. Bam and Linc started looking for the lock again. I walked over to the coffin and noticed that they all had numbers written on them. I can tell that the coffins were Mr. Stone's work, too.

My stomach clenched, but the chain on the fence rattling outside brought me back to reality.

"We've got to go. Now."

"Here it is," Bam held up the lock and key.

Linc snatched it from her, rushed over to the door, and locked it shut with the quickness. I set my lantern down and we all crept to the door of the old barn. We peeked around the door and sneaked out one by one with me being last.

"Hurry, Bri," Bam called out.

Gene and Linc made a packsaddle with their hands so that Bam and I could hop over the fence better. Paul went over then Bam.

"Paul you're bleeding." Bam noticed.

"I know, damned nails on top of de boards," Paul wiped his hand with a leaf.

"Here comes Mr. Stone riding hard this way," Bam warned.

"Come on, y'all gotsta' hurry," Paul added.

Linc, Gene, and I looked at each other.

"We gone have to jump it," I said to both of them.

"You reckon we'll make it?" Gene hesitated.

109

"Yeah, we have to," Linc assured Gene.

"Come on y'all he's getting closer," Bam whispered through the fence.

Gene walked a few paces back then took off running. He jumped and his finger landed in the right spots on the boards.

Up and over, he made it.

"You first cousin." Linc beckoned me to go.

I took a few steps back, ran then jumped. Up and over, I made it. We all peeked between the boards to watch Linc.

Mr. Stone's stench was getting stronger.

"What are y'all chillens' doing here? You know you shouldn't be nowhere near this fence," Mr. Stone barked.

We all mounted our horses. Mr. Stone noticed that one horse was missing a rider.

"Who's…?" Mr. Stone pointed at Jacks.

All of a sudden, Linc flew over the fence and landed dead smack on his saddle.

We all took off riding.

"I'm gonna get y'all. Stay away from this fence," Mr. Stone yelled.

We rode sharply through the woods.

The path, imbrued on our brains. Linc fell off to the side of his steed. Bam knew something was wrong. We caught Linc's steed to the corner of the river where the water was shallow.

Bam hopped down first, then Paul, then Gene and me. Linc was bleeding profusely from his middle part. Bam ripped her top and rushed to cover Linc's middle.

"Oh my God, it won't stop, it won't stop," Bam panicked.

Linc slumped over in pain.

"Here Bam use dis'," Gene ripped off a piece of his top. Bam took the cloth and pressed it up against Linc's middle. He moaned in pain.

"What is we gone do?" Bam said frantically.

My mind started circling. The only person that I knew could fix this came to mind. Lilly.

"Let's take him to Lilly's she'll know what to do."

Paul reached for Linc. Bam started to cry.

"Look at him Bri, he can't ride." Bam leaned on her horse.

"I'll ride him," Gene said. "And I'll ride next to him for support," Paul mounted his horse.

We all hoisted Linc up onto the back of Gene's horse. Linc vomited off to the side.

"What do we do with his horse?" Paul questioned.

"Don't worry 'bout that, I'll take him," I responded.

Everyone was okay with that although they didn't say it. They knew I had a way of getting out of trouble, except with Mamma, of course. I planned to take Linc's horse to our stable and stick him in the back of the barn.

I decided to double back past the fence on my way before the sun went hiding. I used the extra string under my saddle to loop Jacks to Hadie. I slowed Hadie and Jacks as I crept closer to the fence. I saw the nail that nicked Linc because a piece of his flesh was hanging from it.

Apparently, Mr. Stone had not left because his horse, Hank, was standing tied to a tree. By this time, it was completely dark outside. I heard someone tussling closer to the gate. I tied Hadie and Jack to a tree off a-ways so that Mr. Stone wouldn't see. As I crept closer to the gate, something kept hitting me in the head. *PING* from above. I bent over and picked up an acorn. I looked up in the tree. It was Jholie. She beckoned me to climb the tree.

I did.

When I reached her and looked out, I hadn't realized how much could be seen from up here. The view stretched farther than I'd ever imagined, revealing secrets hidden in plain sight.

Down by the schoolhouse, I spotted what looked like Mamma, Deddy, Mr. Smalls, Mr. Stone, and the body of a woman lying limp with a pouch strapped to her front.

My heart dropped as I watched Deddy stuff the woman into a long sack, black and heavy, nothing like the cotton sacks I was used to seeing. Without hesitation, Mr. Smalls and Deddy heaved the covered body into the back of his carriage. Deddy passed something small and shiny to Mr. Stone before he and Mamma mounted their horses and trailed behind Mr. Smalls, leaving a cloud of dust in their wake.

From our perch, we followed Mr. Stone with our eyes as he walked toward the old barn behind the schoolhouse. He reached for the key hanging from the chain around his neck, unlocked the gate, and disappeared inside. Moments later, he reemerged with something bundled tightly in a cloth.

As he carefully unwrapped the cloth, I gasped softly. Nestled inside was a newborn baby with a pale complexion, wiggling and crying. He looked at the baby unusually, pleased like it was some prize he'd just won, an eerie smile crept across his face. He glanced around, as if checking for prying eyes, then hurriedly wrapped the baby back in the cloth, secured it to his saddle, and rode off at a gallop.

I climbed down as much of the tree as I could before I made a big jump for it. I begged Jholie to come with me. I thought that she could ride Linc's horse for safekeeping if we got caught. I could come up with something faster if Jholie was with me. Although she was reluctant to move, she finally relented.

"You owe me. Uhh! Look at all this blood," Jholie said.

"Okay, I owe you. Now would you com'on?" I rushed.

We gathered the horses, Jholie hopped on Jacks and I mounted Hadie. We rode off to our stables. We made it safely. We put the horses in the back stable and closed the barn darn without anyone noticing us.

"Jholie, what did you see back dere'." I turned to Jholie as I closed the barn door.

"First, let me say that y'all are dumb as hell. What were y'all doing in dat' old barn?" Jholie swung her finger in the air.

"Jholie just tell me," I threw my

hands to the side.

"Well, Mr. Stone had just left dere' before y'all pulled up. He dropped off some food and stuff wrapped in a blanket. All I heard him say was, I'll be back for you, den' he walked off. Den' you fools pull up and go in for a long time. What was y'all doing in dere'?" Jholie paused.

"I'll tell you later. Get to de' part where you see Deddy and Mamma," I said.

"While y'all was in dere, Deddy, Mamma, and Mr. Smalls rode up. Deddy opened de gate and dey go into de' back of de' schoolhouse. Dat's when de' drums sounded and y'all came pouring out of dat' barn. One by one over de' fence until Mr. Stone showed up. Den' all of a sudden, Linc comes flying over de' gate and y'all leave. Mr. Stone goes into de' barn and rushes back out. He heads over to de' gate where Deddy, Mamma, and Mr. Smalls were standing. Dey' come out and walk back in. Mr. Smalls had a rope tied to a woman carrying a sack. Den' Mr. Stone walked up and saw it. Mr. Smalls started to tussle wi' Mr. Stone until Deddy broke dem' up.

116

Dat's when you showed back up, sneaking around. You know Mamma is gone' have your hide for dis' one," Jholie remarked.

I looked off into the distance. I could see Meema walking towards us in a frenzy. I had to get myself together.

"Bri, I need to have a word with ya."

Meema looked at Jholiie. "Alone," Meema added. Jholie runs off.

"Yeah, Meema," I said.

"What happened, tonight?" Meema asked.

"What you mean, Meema?" I tried to play it off.

"Girl, don't lie to me. Linc almost bled to death over at Lilly's," Meema walked up on me.

"Is he okay?" I exhaled.

Meema could see the tears in my eyes.

"He's gonna make it, but he probably won't ever have kids." Meema sighed.

I let my tears go; Meema grabbed me and hugged me tightly.

"Bri? Bri, why are you shaking?"

Meema held me tighter.

Words failed me. Meema didn't press.

117

She simply took my hand, her touch steady and knowing, and led me into the house.

She led me to my room without a word, handed me my nightclothes, and I climbed in bed for the night. Meema knows me better than anyone does and I knew the moment would come when I'd have to speak, just not under this moon. She kissed me on my head and tiptoed out of my room, allowing the quiet to settle around me.

CHAPTER 10

The Day After the Festival

I was late to rise, Jholie shaking me gently through the covers. Everyone was already seated at the table except Deddy. The weight of exhaustion from the festival was palpable. The silence filled the air, loud and unyielding. Mamma rose from her chair to make her usual mark on the stick. I slid into the seat next to Meema, who was already busy fixing my plate.

"Thanks, Meema," I reached for my fork.

"Morning," Deddy greeted as he finally emerged from the room, rubbing the sleep from his eyes.

"Hey, Deddy," Jholie and I said in

unison.

"Morning, Son," Meema chimed in after us.

"Morning, Baby," Mamma added as she sat back down.

Deddy sat down at his usual spot. Mamma started fixing his plate. Mamma scooped a spoonful of eggs from inside a cast-iron skillet onto his plate. The golden piles of goodness were accented by; pineapple, grapes, and honeydew melon. On occasion, she'd take a handful of breadcrumbs, crush them, and sprinkle them all over the entire plate.

Meema always said you could tell a lot about a person just by looking at their plate. Mamma reached over and set the plate in front of Deddy. He leaned in for a kiss.

"I thought the festival was nice," Mamma said with a quick peck on Deddy's lips.

"Me, too. Our guests were impressed with your riding Bri. And Baby, they loved the food. They couldn't get enough," Deddy smiled.

"Thanks, Deddy," I said, blushing.

"I heard that Linc got hurt pretty bad, too," Deddy said, breaking the brief pause.

"Yeah, they said the boy almost bled out," Meema added, her tone heavy.

"Ooh, that serious huh?" Mamma asked, glancing toward Meema.

"Serious enough. Elve, Lilly's momma, says Linc might not be able to have kids now, but she ain't told him," Meema said, coughing uncontrollably after finishing her sentence.

Mamma rushed over, patting her back.

"You alright, Momma?" Deddy was already up, dipping a cup into the freshwater bin before setting it down in front of Meema.

"Thank you, baby," Meema sipped the water.

"That bad, huh? I wonder if Rufus ever told that boy about the frogs and the tadpoles," Deddy talked with his mouth full.

"What about frogs and tadpoles, Deddy? Jholie asked innocently.

121

"Talk to ya' Mamma." Deddy replied hastily.

"Speaking of kids, when is Pat expecting?" Mamma shifted her attention.

"Pat is having a baby, too?" I blurted out.

"What you mean, too?" Mamma shot me a sharp glance, her eyes narrowing.

I had to think quickly, but it had to be something that I would naturally say. I just didn't feel like arguing with her today.

Thinking fast, I stuffed a forkful of eggs into my mouth. "Didn't mean nothin' by it. It just slipped."

"Her momma said sometime during the cold season." Mamma said wiping her mouth.

"I don't feel good." I pushed my chair back. "Excuse me, I'm gonna go lay down."

I got up from the table. I could feel their eyes on my back. I walked into my room, plopped down on the bed, and buried myself under the covers. I left the door open and heard Jholie talking to Deddy.

"Deddy can I be excused?" she asked.

"Where you headed?" He asked in return.

"To feed de' horses," she said, already standing.

"Go on baby," Deddy swung his fork in her direction.

Jholie walked into our room and closed the door behind her.

"Bri," Jholie whispered. "I'm about to walk Jacks back to Linc's before Deddy sees him. He's still covered in blood."

I didn't budge.

I felt guilty because I knew I would be in a ton of mess if I was caught and here I was dragging Jholie right along with me.

Jholie left.

I didn't want to think about yesterday. I stayed still, the side of my head pounding in rhythm with my thoughts. So many pieces of yesterday were scattered and blurry. I don't remember how I got back to the house.

From my room, I could hear the creak

of the table as Deddy sat back down to finish his coffee.

"Is our problem gone?" Mamma's voice carried softly through the house.

"Gone and out of our hair," Deddy replied.

"That's good," Meema murmured in agreement.

The clatter of dishes came next as Mamma began clearing the table.

"Meema, go rest yourself," she said gently, noticing the older woman stifling another cough.

"I'm alright, Baby," Meema replied, as she moved slowly toward her rocking chair by the window. She picked up her mending, her fingers working methodically through the fabric.

As the morning gave way to midday, the sun climbed higher, spilling golden light through the windows. Jholie returned, her boots coated in mud and hay.

"Got the horses fed," she announced, leaning her weight against the doorframe.

"And I cleared the troughs, too.

Mamma turned to her, one eyebrow raised. "You clean that room, yet?"

"Not yet, but I'll get to it before sundown," Jholie assured.

Mamma sighed but didn't press further.

"Good. Help your Meema hang those linens when you've caught your breath," Mamma added.

The day stretched on lazily.

I knew Jholie hated the fact that Mamma left me alone and made her do my chores. Mamma worked at a steady pace, churning butter and kneading dough for fresh bread. Deddy headed to the stables in the late afternoon, his tools clinking faintly as he fiddled with something too far off to be seen. Meema napped in her chair for a while before rousing and muttering about the light shining too bright and the linens needing mending.

Outside, the horses stirred, and the chickens squawked, a sign that Jholie had reached the barn to retrieve chicken eggs. Mamma wiped the table, the damp rag smudging remnants of breadcrumbs

and stray coffee rings before she tended
to herself.

"Jholie needs to be quick with
those chickens before the sun gets too
hot," she yelled, as she heard Deddy
walking back into the house.

Deddy leaned back in his chair,
sipping his second cup of coffee, his
eyes half-lidded with lingering fatigue.
After a long moment of silence, he stood
and stretched.

"I'm headed back to the barn for a
spell," he said casually, though the
weight in his tone made Mamma glance up
from her washing.

"Everything alright?" she asked,
wiping her hands on the towel

"Fine," Deddy replied, tipping his
hat before heading out the door.

The sun was just beginning its
descent, the sky streaked with pale
orange and lavender hues. Deddy's boots
crunched on the dry earth as he made his
way to the barn. Inside, the air was
thick with the familiar scent of hay and
animals, but something felt… off.

He moved toward the horses' stalls, his sharp eyes scanning the space. Near the back wall, where Jacks had been tied earlier, his gaze snagged on a patch of darkened hay. Squatting down, he reached out and brushed his fingers over the stain. His hand came away sticky and red.

Deddy stood slowly, his face a mask of unreadable calm, though the tightening of his jaw betrayed his thoughts. The streaks of dried blood trailed faintly toward the door, as if someone had made a hurried attempt to clean but hadn't thought to check the hay.

He didn't move for a moment, the barn silent except for the low shuffle of a horse pawing at the ground. Then, as though satisfied with his silent assessment, Deddy turned and left the barn, letting the door creak shut behind him.

Back at the house, Mamma glanced up as he returned.

"Find everything in order out there?" she asked, setting a pot of greens onto the stove.

"Mostly," he said, brushing a hand against his shirt. "Just noticed a mess that needs tending to."

"You want me to send Jholie back out?"

"No. I'll take care of it in the morning," Deddy replied. He leaned down to kiss the top of her head.

"You sit and rest," Mamma suggested then nodded.

The way Deddy's hand lingered at his belt as he stood near the door made it clear his thoughts weren't at ease.

By the time supper rolled around, the smell of greens, smoked ham, and cornbread wafted through the house. Jholie set the table, carefully placing knives and forks, while Mamma dished out portions onto heavy wood plates.

As we ate, some of the day's heaviness eased slightly. Meema talked about how the neighbor's dog chased the chickens, sending everyone into laughter. Deddy leaned back in his chair, tapping the table absentmindedly, but his expression softened every time Mamma passed him the salt or filled his glass. When Jholie spoke his eyes stiffened.

After the plates were cleared, I helped Jholie dry the dishes while Mamma stitched a small tear in one of her skirts.

There was a knock at the door.

Jholie rushed to see who it was. To her surprise it was Micha standing on the other side of it.

"Mamma can go over to Micha's? I won't be long," she asked.

"Not long after its dark, I spect' to see you coming through that door," Mamma said sharply.

The sky outside had faded into inky black, and the coolness of the evening crept through the open window. I returned to my soft place, under my sheets.

The quiet of exhaustion soon blanketed the house. One by one, I heard doors shutting as everyone retreated to their rooms. Then came the squeal of the side door—it had to be Jholie. Her steps fumbled before she finally made her way back into our room. She quickly washed

and then changed into her nightclothes
and dropped onto her bed.

"Bri you woke?" She whispered.

I was up, but I didn't want to talk
or move, so I didn't respond. I didn't
make a sound. I stayed silent, feigning
sleep.

"On my walk over to Micha's, I
heard a baby crying and I thank it was
coming from Mr. Stone's house. And I know
you can hear me. Don't forget…you owe
me," Jholie sighed, then pulled the
covers over her head, and soon drifted
off.

Underneath the candlelight of the
moon, Slope snuggled up against the warm
river and was quiet for the night.

Far out on the horizon, Mr. Smalls'
ship was just a shadow against the sea,
its faint outline barely visible through
the thickening mist. Onboard, a crew of
fourteen worked quietly, with the
occasional grumble breaking the eerie
calm.

Below deck, locked in a cramped

cabin, the white woman taken from Slope sat in the suffocating dark.

Mrs. Smalls descended the creaking stairs with measured steps. In her hand, a rusty lantern cast flickering light against the damp wooden walls. She stopped outside the cabin door, her expression unreadable as she knocked hard, the sound reverberating through the corridor.

"I don't need nothin'," came the hoarse voice from behind the door.

"Good," Mrs. Smalls snapped, her tone laced with contempt. "I ain't a slave checking on my mistress," Mrs. Small's snapped. "Just seeing if you still breathing. Not that I'd lose sleep if you weren't. Can't wait to get rid of you."

A hollow laugh followed from the other side of the door.

"Do whatever you gonna do. I don't care no more," the voice agreed.

Mrs. Smalls scowled, muttering under her breath as she turned and made her way back up to the main deck. As she

stepped into the fresh air, Mr. Smalls
caught sight of her from the wheel. He
tipped his hat back, his mouth curling
into a faint smirk as he approached her.

"Well?"

"Well, what?" she retorted, brushing
past him.

"How is she?" Mr. Smalls pressed,
following her movements with sharp eyes.

"She's alive," Mrs. Smalls answered
curtly.

Mr. Smalls chuckled, low and
guttural.

"When we getting rid of her and her
baby?" Mrs. Smalls asked, crossing her
arms. Her voice held no sympathy, only
impatience as she walked to their cabin
with him close behind.

"Not tonight," he said with a
dismissive wave. "We got smooth waters
ahead, and I aim to enjoy it. Thought I
might let the men have a bit of sport
before we deal with her... and the babe."

Mrs. Smalls narrowed her eyes, but
she said nothing, staring at her
husband's weathered face. The lantern

light reflected in his eyes as he pulled her closer by the waist.

"Ain't heard no crying," she said suddenly, her tone sharp.

"What's that?" Mr. Smalls asked.

"The baby," she clarified, her voice more insistent. "I ain't heard no crying since we set off."

Mr. Smalls shrugged, unbothered.

"Maybe it's sleepin'. Maybe it ain't." He turned his attention to loosening the buttons on his shirt.

Mrs. Smalls tilted her head as if weighing his words.

"I better check," she said, starting to pull away.

"Nah," Mr. Smalls said, catching her arm and spinning her back toward him.

"That can wait. I need you tonight."

She hesitated, but his grip tightened, and the edge of her resistance faded into a hollow smile. He guided her to the bed, his hand firm at her waist.

Behind the locked door at the far end of the corridor, silence hung heavy in the darkness, broken only by the soft, rhythmic creak of the ship against the waves.

CHAPTER 11

The Reveal

This morning, I felt a little more energized, like maybe today could bring some clarity. After breakfast, Jholie and I wandered over to Bam's house. She was standing on the side of her house bent over, sharing her breakfast with the grass. A mixture of stomach acids and eggs.

"What a lovely fragrance, Bam," I joked, wrinkling my nose.

"You alright, Bam?" Jholie acted concerned as she reached out to rub Bam's back.

"Yeah, just fine," she replied dryly, wiping her mouth with the back of her hand.

Bam stood up, walked to her front,

and took a seat on her steps. Jholie and I
sat down beside her. Jholie instantly got
bored with Bam and me, so she journeyed
over to Micah's house right next door.

Bam and I sat still until Mr. Stone
came out from his house carrying what
looked like a bucket of dirty white
cloths. Without a word, he headed toward
the woods and disappeared behind the
trees.

"He been actin' weird lately," Bam
frowned.

"You mean dese' last few days?" I
leaned back, pretending to act casual.

"Yeah, well, we both know why."

"You think he told yo' Mamma and
Deddy 'bout us sneaking in that old barn?"
Bam's voice dropped low, her gaze darting
toward her feet.

I shook my head,

"Nah, and if he did, dey ain't said
nothin' yet," I assured.

Bam's face clouded with worry as she
shifted closer to me.

"I ain't slept right since…," her
voice trembled.

She rested her head on my shoulder, and I instinctively wrapped my arm around her.

"All those coffins," she whispered.

"Why, Bri? Why dey dere? Who dey belong to? Who's rotting away in 'em?"

I sighed deeply, my own unease echoing hers.

"I don't have an answer for you, but I'm gonna find out sooner or later," I assured Bam.

Just then, we heard the sound of twigs snapping under heavy boots. Mr. Stone emerged from the woods, his expression unreadable. For a brief moment, his eyes locked on us, sending a chill crawling up my spine. He wasn't just looking at us; he was staring at all the questions swimming in my head.

"I bet he knows every answer," I said under my breath.

A part of me wanted to march right up to him and demand the truth, but something held me back. It wasn't just fear, I didn't want to pull Bam deeper into whatever this was. She had other things to worry about. Which brought me right back to Linc. I tried to look on the brighter side of things; at least he would have one child if everything goes right.

"Bam, I'll see you later," I said, standing and stretching. "I'm gonna check on Linc."

"I'll go wi'cha'," Bam struggled to her feet, holding out a hand.

I grabbed it to help her up, but she wasn't as steady as I'd hoped. I ended up grabbing her arm, too, to stop her from toppling over.

"Look," I teased with a smirk, "I ain't about to carry you everywhere."

"I am going to need your help," Bam got serious.

"You tell your Momma, yet?" I asked.

"No, I don't know how," Bam said quietly.

As we got closer to Linc's house, Brik exited his cabin. He didn't say anything to us. He just looked, nodded his head, and walked away. We approached the door, but before we could knock, the door opened. It was Linc's mom, Cousin Sherry. Her face was a curious mix of emotions; tears streaming down her cheeks but a strange, radiant smile lit her face.

Behind her, we could hear Linc's voice.

"Let them in Ma," he said, his voice hoarse but steady.

Cousin Sherry moved me aside, reached out, and squeezed the life out of Bam.

"I had to tell her, to stop her from crying bout' my injury," Linc confessed.

Bam dropped her head. I could tell that she was thinking about her Momma, the look on her face said it all. To hear the news from Cousin Sherry's mouth and not her own would crush her Momma.

I thought about my Mamma, too. I knew she'd put two and two together and figure out that I was talking about Bam and Linc when she mentioned Pat. I wasn't looking forward to revisiting that conversation at all.

"She promised she wouldn't tell anyone till she talked to us, first," Linc said.

Bam started crying.

"Why you crying, Bam?" Cousin Sherry rubbed her back.

"I don't know but I know...I mean." Bam started rambling.

Linc struggled to his feet. He hobbled over to Bam and hugged her.

"Look, I know that we are young but I see Slope in your eyes, the best of it. I'd expect everyone would agree that there ain't no better place to be. If I was in a fight, I'd want no one by my side but you." Linc tried to kneel down. Cousin Sherry grabbed his left arm and I grabbed his right. We helped him to the floor, but you could see him trembling on the way down.

He was in pain but pulled himself together, quickly. He pulled a piece of gold string from his pants. He took Bam's finger and tied the string on her ring finger. Bam looked at Linc with tears in her eyes.

"I don't know about the future, alls I know is dat' dere' ain't no future if I can't wake up and know dat' you and our baby..." He reached out at gently rubbed Bam's belly. "I hope he's a boy." He looked up at Bam and stared at her directly in the eyes. "...are staring back at me." His voice was softer than I'd ever heard it.

Linc had a look on his face that Bam nor I have never seen. It could have been from his pain, but it could be something new, something more permanent, something more real.

Bam started crying harder.

"One day, and you don't have to answer nah, but will you be my rib, my other half, my medicine, my wife?" Linc pleaded.

Bam looked back at me.

I couldn't help but to smile. I'd never seen or heard Linc be so serious. It was as if he changed overnight, or the cut on his you know what ripped some sense into him. Either way, this was a good thing. My best friend and my favorite cousin will be one.

I still don't know where this left me. I felt some type of way about all of this, but this wasn't the time nor place.

Tears spilled down Bam's cheeks as she whispered, "Yes, Linc."

Linc stood slowly and pulled Bam closer. They shared a kiss. Cousin Sherry started to cry, again. Her husband, Rufus comforted her.

"We got a lot of plannin' to do," Cousin Sherry said eagerly.

We heard mumbling outside. We all went to their looking whole and saw all the chaos. In an instant, there was a huge fuss outside. We all looked at Cousin Sherry. She looked away, ashamedly.

"Well, I only told a few folks," said Cousin Sherry. "Why didn't you tell your Momma, Bam? I didn't know she didn't know."

Bam exhaled deeply, her shoulders sinking under the weight of the moment. She had known this conversation was inevitable, but she had hoped for more time to find the right words, to gather enough courage, But there Ms. Betty stood, arms crossed, her expression unreadable, waiting.

Bam couldn't meet her mother's eyes at first. She stared at the ground, rubbing her hands together as if the right words might appear between her palms. She had faced storms, long nights of aching worry, and now, the hardest part was confessing the truth.

"Momma, I wanted to tell you," she started, her voice barely above a whisper.

"I just, I didn't know how."

Miss Betty inhaled sharply, "You didn't know how to tell me, but you knew how to let the whole town know?"

Bam winced at the sting in her mother's tone. She wasn't wrong, but it wasn't that simple.

"I was scared, Momma."

Ms. Betty's face softened just a bit, but she didn't move, "Scared of what?"

"Scared of disappointin' you. Of hearin' you say I done ruined myself," Bam admitted, her voice trembling now.

Ms. Betty finally stepped forward, reaching out, but she stopped just short of touching her daughter.

"Bam, baby, I ain't never gonna stop

lovin' you. Ain't no mistake you can make that'll change that. But you shoulda come to me. You ain't gotta do this alone."

Tears welled in Bam's eyes, and before she could stop herself, she closed the space between them. Ms. Betty pulled her into a tight embrace, her warmth sinking into Bam's tired bones.

"I just—" Bam started, but the lump in her throat swallowed the words.

"I know," Ms. Betty said softly. "And listen to me, your Daddy would be proud. You hear me? Proud."

Bam let out a shaky breath, nodding against her mother's shoulder. She wasn't ready, not yet. But maybe, just maybe, she wouldn't have to be.

We looked at Cousin Sherry who started to confess.

"Everyone was all so worried bout Linc's wound. I...I just wanted to spread some joy. And I'm gonna be a grandma," Cousin Sherry added.

We helped Linc outside to find all of the women in Slope standing with cakes and food headed to the mess hall. It was like

they had already planned a feast. I saw
Mamma, Deddy and Meema walking, too.

Meema's nephew, Uncle Rufus, and
some of the younger men walked Linc back
into the house to celebrate.

When we got to the mess hall, there
was a plethora of food leftovers from the
festival. The women who normally do the
cooking warmed everything up and before
you know it, everything was quiet from all
the chewing. I looked around the hall and
noticed that mostly everyone was present
except Mr. Stone.

As the food warmed and the hum of
conversation filled the mess hall, I
couldn't shake the unease brewing in my
chest. People moved around me, sharing
laughs and trading stories, but my eyes
kept darting to the empty seat at the far
end of the room. It belonged to Mr. Stone,
always at the edge, always watching.

Tonight, his absence felt louder than
any of the chatter in the hall.

I tried to focus on Bam and Linc,
sitting together at the center of it all.
Bam's cheeks were flushed with the kind of

joy that doesn't come often, and Linc, even in his weakened state, was smiling like he had the whole world in his hands. Cousin Sherry flitted about, already planning a hundred things for their ceremony, her excitement contagious.

Still, my mind kept wandering. Where was Mr. Stone? What was he doing while the rest of us gathered here? My thoughts spiraled back to the barn, to the rows of coffins that didn't belong, to the questions that kept piling up.

Suddenly, there was a commotion at the back of the hall. Someone spilled a plate, and laughter rippled through the crowd, breaking the tension in the air. I used the distraction to slip outside, needing a moment to clear my head. The cool evening air wrapped around me as I leaned against the wall, staring out at the trees.

Somewhere in the distance, I thought I saw a flicker of movement, quick and deliberate. My stomach twisted, but I forced myself to stay still. If it was Mr. Stone, he didn't want to be seen, and chasing after him now would only make things worse.

The sound of the mess hall doors creaking open behind me pulled me back to the moment. I turned to see Meema stepping out, her eyes wise and heavy with unspoken words. She didn't say anything, just handed me a plate of food and patted my arm.

"Eat, Bri," she said softly. "You can't solve nothing on an empty stomach."

I nodded, but as I followed her back inside, I couldn't shake the feeling that something was shifting, and soon, none of us would be able to ignore it.

As the sun went hiding, the people from Slope congratulated Linc and Bam on their new family and promised them gifts at their ceremony. Cousin Sherry was real pleased but I wasn't. My future was foggy. I had no baby, no relationship, and only one plan. I'd plan to go back to that old barn to see who or what's in those coffins. The only thing that I was certain of was that Bam nor Linc could go with me this time. I wasn't worried, tho.

147

I didn't need them. I only wanted to know one thing. This could have been answered easily, but only by a few folks, none of which were going to tell me. Mr. Stone definitely knows, as does Mamma and Deddy. I wondered if Mr. Smalls knew.

On my way home, I looked out over the dark sea. Mr. Smalls' ship was no longer visible along with his knowledge of that old barn. I began to hurry down our row. I could smell the rain coming.

CHAPTER 12

Storm is Coming

Although morning had come, the sky
clung to its darkness, a smothering black
gray that threatened chaos. Mr. Smalls
stood firm on the quarterdeck, scanning
the horizon. He ordered his crew to open
the sail so that they could use the wind
for a push. A storm was brewing, he could
feel it in the weight of the air and hear
it in the slap of waves against the ship's
hull.

He gave a single nod to his crew, and
they sprang into action, unfurling the
sails to steal the storm's momentum before
it turned hostile. Each wave sent the ship
lurching, forcing the crew into awkward,
stumbling dances as they braced themselves
for what lay ahead.

The feeding crew stood on the edge of
the quarter deck trying to catch the day's
meal before the waters got too bad. The

ladies on the ship gathered dry cloths and prepared the leftovers for breakfast. Mrs. Smalls had a plate for their white passengers ready to deliver. She refused the exact same meal the night before. Mrs. Smalls looked at the plate then spat on it. She gathered the necessary silverware and left the kitchen area. As she left the galley, her gaze found Mr. Smalls on his way back to deck.

"Mornin," she said flatly.

"Mornin, sunshine," he replied, his tone a strange mix of warmth and weariness.

They embraced briefly, and as Mr. Smalls reached for a biscuit from the tray, Mrs. Smalls smacked his hand away.

"Where you headed with that plate."

He looked confused.

"I'm taking it to that ofay," Mrs. Smalls paused. "Why is she still alive?" Mrs. Smalls seemed disgusted. Mr. Smalls dropped his head and stared at his wife in the eyes.

"What is the rush? The sea has had its share of dead bodies to feast on. It can wait for one mo' meal," Mr. Smalls grabbed Mrs. Smalls.

Mrs. Smalls pulled away from him, her displeasure written plainly on her face.

"After you deliver the plate, stay put. Storm is comin' and this one looks angry," Mr. Smalls got serious.

Without waiting for a response, Mrs. Smalls walked the dim corridor. She slowed her pace as she approached the cabin where the white woman was being held. Once she got to the door, she pressed her ear against it and listened for a while.

Silence.

Her heart quickened, with joy and curiosity. She banged on the door, but there was no response. Narrowing her eyes, she pushed the door open, the hinges creaking like a warning. Inside, the white woman was hanging like a chandelier from a board in the ceiling; barely breathing with a necklace of bedsheets tied tightly around her neck. Her body swayed gently, as the blush on her skin turned pale. Mrs. Smalls tilted her head, watching the scene with detached curiosity. She sat on a stool near the door, crossed her legs, and inspected her fingernails.

"I'll wait," Mrs. Smalls murmured.

At that moment, the white woman's eyes began to roll in the top of her head. Mrs. Smalls finally got up and slowly left the cabin to search for Mr. Smalls. She found Mr. Smalls in his quarters, bent over a map.

"Bobby," she said calmly, "that bitch hanged herself. She solved the problem for us. Have the men toss her body."

Mr. Smalls bolted upright and rushed past her toward the cabin. He flung the door open and froze. He sees her, pre-lifeless body, hanging from a board in the ceiling. She hanged there, her breath shallow but present. His mind flashed back for a moment and without a thought, he rushed over, took a blade from his pocket, and cut her down. He started pressing on her chest over and over again. The woman convulsed, then let out a deep, agonizing breath, followed by violent coughs. Mrs. Smalls entered the room and grabbed her husband's shoulders.

"What are you doing?" Mrs. Smalls hissed.

Mr. Smalls panted as he looked up at Mrs. Smalls. The white woman finally caught her breath and turned on her side. Without looking in her direction, Mrs. Smalls gave the white woman one last kick in the back. The white woman screamed in agony.

"Not time yet," Mr. Smalls slurred.

"When will it be time?" Mrs. Smalls snapped. She turned and stormed out of the room, her frustration simmering.

"Just check on the baby!" Mr. Smalls yelled.

In a mad rage, Mrs. Smalls stomps around the room.

"Where is the baby bitch?" Mrs. Smalls rummaged through some quilts on the cot. She raised the pillow, walked over to the chair, and removed the throw. The white woman gathered herself and kneeled. She looked at Mr. Smalls then at Mrs. Smalls. With a mouth full of blood, spat, and let out a treacherous laugh.

Mrs. Smalls walked over to her and

smacked her in the mouth. Blood trickled down the side of the white woman's face, as she continued to bellow out a teasing laugh.

Mr. Smalls stood up.

Mrs. Smalls grabbed the white woman around the neck as she choked for air. Mr. Smalls grabbed Mrs. Smalls, snatching her away. She finally released the white woman, leaving deep red marks tattooed around her neck.

Using the only strength she had left, the white woman sat up.

"You think you're so smart don'tcha'. Well, guess what? It ain't here. And if you wouldn'ov been so nosy, I wouldn't be here either. You should'a let me die," the white woman scowled.

"Did you kill'it?" Mr. Smalls went over to the cot and rummaged through the covers. A look of pure awe covered the face of Mr. Smalls. The white woman started to cry. Mrs. Smalls had had enough and stormed out of the cabin.

Mr. Smalls noticed the uneaten plate of food. He walked over to it and picked it up. He looked at the white woman bellowing on the floor. He placed the uneaten plate of food beside her.

"Eat," he ordered.

She grabbed his arm before he rose.

"Why...Why didn't you let me die?"

The white woman released Mr. Smalls' arm.

Their eyes met for the first time. For a moment, he didn't answer. Then he turned away, his expression unreadable. He headed for the door but paused before exiting.

"Eat," Mr. Smalls pushed the food closer to her.

The white woman looked at Mr. Smalls one last time before she snatched her hair from her face. Outside the cabin, Mrs. Smalls waited, her footsteps pacing the narrow hall.

"I told you we should'a got rid of her the first day," she snapped when he emerged.

"We got bigger problems now," he replied. Forget all that nah, we gots to find this baby," Mr. Smalls responded.

155

"What baby? She kill'd dat baby jus' like she was tryin' to kill hersef'," Mrs. Smalls wiped her forehead. "What mo' do you need to know."

Mr. Smalls hesitated, his eyes drifting toward the closed cabin door where his feet were soon to follow. He no longer heard her cries. Instead, he heard the sound of eating.

All of a sudden, the ship groaned under the weight of a monstrous wave, slamming both of them against the walls of the corridor. Mr. Smalls grabbed his wife.

"Get to our cabin. Stay put. Storm's here, and I don't need you goin' overboard. "I'll be there when I can," Mr. Small's demanded.

Mrs. Smalls hesitated, then nodded and disappeared down the dim hall. Mr. Smalls remained where he was, staring at the door behind which the woman sat. For the first time, he felt the weight of something deeper than the storm pressing down on them all.

CHAPTER 13

The Teachings

School was starting again, and the buzz of anticipation hung in the air. Miss Jones had just unloaded her cart, summoning Gene and Paul to help her carry the load. They were obliged to do it.

The way Meema told it, Miss Jones risked her freedom every season to bring us books and supplies from the far corners of the world. She spent the scorching months riding through hostile lands, surviving on scraps or whatever she could hunt. Meema said she'd never once seen her at a festival. Miss Jones was always gone during that time. Meema described her like a shadowy hero, a vigilante in

petticoats, always on the run, stealing
information for us from the most
unwelcoming places. Miss Jones's great-
great-grandmother was born into to
captivity, but had escaped and found
Slope.

"Show her respect," Meema would say.
"She's got the blood of teachers in her
veins. She comes from a long line of
teachers. Her momma's momma's momma was
the first teacher in Slope," Meema went
on. "Everything that we know about the
outside world, we owe to the Jones'."

The weight of that legacy clung to
Miss Jones like a second skin. But the
Jones family's legacy was not without its
ghosts, either.

Meema told us about one hot season,
long before I was born, when one of the
Jones' women left with her crew on a usual
mission. None of them ever came back. When
school time rolled around and the group
still hadn't returned, a search party was
sent out. Days turned into weeks with no
sign of them. It just so happened that on
the ride back through the Midwest, one of

the searchers stopped to relieve himself underneath the shade of an American Elm tree.

As he was doing his business, he looked up to the sky with relief and saw what was left of her lifeless body hanging from the tree, swaying in the wind like a grim pendulum.

By that time, there was almost nothing left, just bones and a few pieces of rotten flesh that scavengers left behind. The only way they knew it was her was because there were remnants from a scarf made by her momma tied around her arm. The searchers decided to make a mark in that old tree and bury her right underneath it. The body was just too fragile for the journey home.

I supposed everyone in Slope knows that story, a reminder of the dangers the Jones women faced and the price they paid. Knowing this, helped me to understand why Miss Jones don't take no mess. I figured the only way to respect what she has done is for us to pay attention and do what I was told. I didn't say I liked it at all, but I respected the fact that she put her life on the line for my knowledge.

I loved arithmetic and reading which is why it saddened me to think that my last session of school was so close. This would be my last chance to learn all that I could from Miss Jones.

We all met outside of Bam's house before nightfall, just to catch up. It was the evening before school and we were all anxious minus Pat and Jaks. They were done with school and were required to take on normal routines during the day like the other grown-ups in Slope. I was told that Pat and Jaks did little work but a lot of panting and sweating in the shed during the day.

Gene and Paul showed off their new satchels that Gene's momma made for them. Jholie and Micha argued about which dress to wear in the morning, which I thought was a foolish argument. If it were up to me, none of us would wear dresses at all. And looking at Bam she was going to need all new dresses, two sizes bigger than normal.

Bam sat on the porch, her belly so large it looked like she'd swallowed a barrel. Mr. Stone worked nearby, carving what seemed to be a baby's crib.

Everyone guessed it was for Bam and Linc, though with so many expectant bellies in Slope, no one could say for sure. Still, Bam acted like she didn't know, but you could see her excitement in the way her eyes lingered on the wood.

I couldn't help worrying about how she'd fit into the schoolhouse desk. Her belly already looked like it was plotting a mutiny against the rest of her body. I took it upon myself to go and ask Miss Jones about where Bam would sit but that did not go as planned.

"Mornin' Miss Jones, de' first day is almost here and dere…,"--

Before I could even get the words out, Miss Jones cut me off.

"You're too old to be talking like a child, Bri," she said, her voice sharp as the edge of a ruler. "Your words have weight now. They influence others. Don't waste them."

I wasn't in the mood for a lecture, but out of respect for Miss Jones I stood there until she was finished. At the end of her rant, I politely walked away. Her words stung. All I wanted was to help Bam, but instead, I felt scolded. I didn't go there for that.

Here I was, trying to do something right and I got chewed out for it. I rushed back over to Bam's house.

"What you hiding in dere'? A watermelon? You know if you was hungry all you gotta' do is say som'n."

I high- fived Linc who was standing next to Bam. Bam made a valiant attempt at chasing me, but she easily gave up after she realized her belly wouldn't let her.

"I gotta tell you somethin', Bri," she said, looking at the ground.

"Yeah, what?" I asked, suddenly uneasy.

"I ain't going to school wich'ya dis season." Her voice was soft, but her words hit like a thunderclap. Bam looked up.

I froze. "Why not?"

162

"Momma supposes dat' I might be like one of dose' ladies dat' have more dan', one baby, at a time. She says dat' my belly is just too big for me to be only caring one. But Miss Sherry says dat' Linc was de' size of a toddler when he came out. She said he barely made it out, too," Bam's worry was written all over her face as she lowered herself onto the porch steps.

For the first time, I noticed how tired she looked, how heavy her movements had become. I sat beside her, unsure of what to say, and stared out at the darkening horizon where storm clouds were gathering, the first whispers of wind brushing through the trees.

She knew what she would be missing by not going to school. I knew how she felt. I was already missing it. I was going to learn all that I could before the end. I still planned on riding around the world on Hadie. And since I'd be alone, I wanted to do it like a vigilante. The way Ms. Jones tells it, there's lots to see. I was even thinking about making a stop by that tree.

"Hey, I'll learn for all three of us. And your first lesson is quit saying dat, dem, and dere. Miss Jones said that we are saying it wrong. You have to put your tongue right up against your front teeth and pronounce the words like that, them, there, nothing, and something."

"Really, Bri?" Bam was not convinced.

"Yeah. See I am smarter *than* you already," I cracked.

She smiled.

That next morning, one-by-one, the youngins' of Slope poured out of their homes, all heading toward the schoolhouse. I stood among them, waiting for Miss Jones to open the heavy wooden doors. When they finally creaked open, she stood in the doorway, her sharp eyes scanning the crowd before ushering us in with a firm gesture.

The schoolhouse was decorated beautifully. The room was alive with color and wonder, decorated with artifacts and objects I had never seen before. Every detail seemed deliberate,

each item placed to catch our attention.
The younger kids were wide-eyed, their
whispers echoing through the room as they
tried to guess the purpose of the strange
gadgets. Even Jholie, who was hard to
impress, seemed captivated.

"I don't think Miss Jones slept the
night before," I whispered in my head. It
seemed like she was just as eager as we
were to get started and by the looks of
the classroom, it must've taken all night
to set this up.

"Come on in, everyone. Take a seat,"
she said, her voice crisp but welcoming.
"Youngest in the front, oldest in the
back."

Jholie darted to the very front,
plopping down as if the spot had been
reserved for her.

"Not so fast, Jholie," Miss Jones
said, pointing to a seat farther back.
"You're older now. That seat's for the
littlest ones."

Grumbling, Jholie got up and took
the seat closest to Micah, casting a
sideways glance at the younger kids who

now claimed the front row. It became
routine to let the youngins' sit first so
that we wouldn't have to fuss with all of
the confusion to find a spot.

Once everyone was seated, Miss Jones
walked to her desk and picked up an
object. The object looked like a perfect
circle, placed diagonally on a cast iron
stand. It was full of color but mostly
blue. Miss Jones sat it back down on her
desk and spun it around. It whirled until
she placed her finger back on it, which
brought it to a halting stop.

"Does anyone know what this is?" she
asked, holding the object up for us all to
see.

The room stayed quiet, all eyes on
Brik, who usually answered first. But
this time, he stayed silent.

Unexpectedly, Omar, one of the
youngest, raised his hand.

"Yes, Omar," Miss Jones prompted.

"It's a circle," Omar motioned with
his hands.

The older kids chuckled. Miss Jones's
head rose. Her eyes zapped through

166

everyone with a smirk on their face. The room got quiet.

"You are right, little Omar, and quite brave for raising your hand to answer. It is a circle. Does everyone see that?" Miss Jones picked up the object.

Miss Jones looked around the room to survey for those that were not responding or had silly looks on their faces.

She paused, turning the object in her hands so all could get a good view. Then, she continued, "But this isn't just any circle. It's a very special one. This is called a globe."

I raised my hand. Miss Jones pointed at me.

"What is a globe, Miss Jones?" I asked with my hand still in the air.

"Well, a good question," she replied with a smile. "All students, take out a sheet of paper and pencil from inside of the desk. Listen to my instructions carefully, I want the younger students to draw a circle on their paper, as big as you all can make it. Older students, please come to my desk to have a closer look."

"Do we bring our paper with us?" Paul blurted out, without raising his hand.

"Not you, Paul," Miss Jones said with a sharp look. "You didn't raise your hand. Have a seat."

Out of the corner of my eye, I see Linc's arm shoot in the air. I couldn't wait for Miss Jones to call on him. I knew he would say something that was gonna land him cleaning up slop by the chicken coop. Miss Jones finally pointed at Linc. Linc straightened his back then cleared his throat.

"Miss Jones, would you like for us to bring our paper?" Linc smirked then looked at Brik.

"No, everyone, please bring your closed mouth that is attached to your body." Miss Jones gently set the globe down on her desk then stood to the side. The older students popped up, almost instantaneously, and approached the desk.

We were obedient.

"Tell me, what you see," she said.

"I see North America," Brik eyes

quickly.

"Miss Jones ain't dat where we at?" TJ adds.

"Yes, *that* is where we are. One quick thing. I must add a very important side note. This should be easy to grasp, although we will work on this more often; Pay attention to how you speak.

One thing I learned in all my travels is people will judge you based on how you look and speak. Words like *dem*, *dere*, *dat*, and *dis*, we're leaving them behind. The proper words are *them*, *there*, *that*, and *this*. Isn't that right, Bri?" Miss Jones stood at her chalkboard writing out the words.

Caught off guard, I looked away and nodded even though she wasn't looking.

"Now you all try it. Press your tongue against your front teeth and try it," she paused, letting her words sink in.

"Now, speaking of the world, this is in fact a Globe, and Brik was right; this big mass is North America," Miss Jones pointed to a mass on the globe.

"Hey, look at this. This is shaped like the necklace that my Daddy wears around his neck. He calls it the Motherland." Paul added.

"Very observant, Paul. But the official name for the country is Africa. It is said to be the first home to all men. It is where we all are from. Return to your seats." Miss Jones shooed us back to our seats.

"Now, on your paper, answer this question." Miss Jones walked to her desk and removed a piece of chalk. She walked over to the board and wrote:

What is a globe?

"Write this question on your paper just as you see it. After you have finished writing the question, answer it, then share your answer with a neighbor." She walked from around her desk.

"And for my younger students, bring your body and your circle to my desk in a single file line," she directed.

As we wrote, the younger kids scurried up to get in line. One-by-one they approached the globe for a closer

look. And one-by-one Miss Jones asked them
if their circle looked like the shape of a
globe. Those that got Miss Jones's
approval were instructed to help the ones
who didn't. I looked over at Linc and saw
him staring out of the window.

"Coz, you alright?" I whispered.

"Yeah, I was wondering what she was
doing," Linc muttered, his head resting
lazily on the desk.

"Linc and Bri, since you two have so
much to say, stand and enlighten everyone:
What is a globe?" Miss Jones instructed.

We both stood at the same time.

"A globe is a picture of places,
drawn on a circle," I offered confidently.

"Naw, it ain't," Linc interrupted,
his tone bordering on smug.

"A globe is a circle with shapes of
the world on it," Linc looked proud.

"What's the difference, fool?" I shot
back, narrowing my eyes at him.

"Yours just said, picture of places,"
he pushed my shoulder.

We went back and forth for a spell
until Miss Jones intervened.

"You're both right, in a way," she said, her tone firm. "And Linc, keep your hands to yourself, or I'll let the elder men deal with you."

Her yardstick shifted toward us like a warning. "Now, older students, write this down: *A globe is a circular representation of the Earth.*" Brik's hand shot up in the air, and Miss Jones pointed at him.

"Miss Jones, you telling us that this thing we live on is shaped like a circle and not flat like a flapjack?" Brik lowered his hand.

"That is exactly what I am saying, Brik," Miss Jones responded.

Just then, the sound of Old Man Eddie's bell rang out from the mess hall.

"Time for lunch," Miss Jones announced, placing the globe back on her desk. "We'll continue this after you've all had your meal."

The class scrambled toward the mess hall, eager for the midday break. Everyone but Brik, that is, who darted off toward his house, disappearing into the woods.

By now, the trees were dense and wild, their branches laden with vines and moss. On the way out of the door, Linc, Paul, and Gene nudged my arm for me to stay back a minute.

"So I guess you done with *this* schoolhouse and *that* old barn?" Linc teased.

"Did you just say *this* and *that*?" I asked, raising an eyebrow.

"Yeah. Bam already told me. She thinks we should raise a smart child and I agree," Linc sighed.

Linc, you da' last person that should be talking 'bout that old barn." Gene grabbed his middle.

"Wells' I ain't. I ain't get this

scar for nothin'," slightly lowering his britches below his waistline. "I wanna know what is in those coffins," Linc added.

"We all do, but we gotta' to be smart about findin' out," I patted Linc on the shoulder.

Miss Jones came to the front of the schoolhouse and shut the doors.

"Y'all go on ahead," I said to the others. "I'll catch up later."

As they walked off, I turned back to the schoolhouse and knocked gently. After a pause, the door opened. Miss Jones stood there, her mouth full of food. She raised a single finger, motioning for patience as she finished chewing. She finally finished chewing.

"Yes Bri, what can I do for you?"

Miss Jones stood holding the door opened.

"I was wonderin' if I could talk to you for a moment," I asked hesitantly.

"Well, I guess so, but don't let this be an everyday thing, I like to eat alone." She beckoned for me to sit down.

"Oh, no Mam it won't be," I assured her.

"Well, have a seat." She welcomed me.

I took a seat at the desk closest to hers. She looked at me and waited for my mouth to start moving, but I was in a trance. Sitting there, close to her in awe, I'd never noticed all the scratches and bruises that lay upon her skin. I can

174

tell she saw me looking at them because
she tightened the scarf around her neck
and draped her shawl over her shoulders. I
wondered if that was the scarf that Meema
spoke of. It sparkled blue when the sun
hit it.

"Miss Jones, my Meema told me that
you been all over the world and seen a lot
of things," I was enthused.

"She'd be right, Bri," she replied
softly.

"Well, that's what I want to do too."

Her lips curved into a small smile.

"You want to be a teacher, Bri?" She
asked.

"No, Mam. I just want to see the
world," I said.

She nodded thoughtfully, "Oh, I see.
Well, Bri I would say take your time. The
world can be an ugly place for people that
look like you and me just because we look
the way we look and no other reason."

"I know Mam, Meema tells me all kinds
of stories about the world...How did you
make it through...lookin' how you look in
all?"

Her expression darkened slightly, and she looked away. "Bri it wasn't easy. I had to go undercover like a spy, almost."

"A spy?" I repeated, intrigued.

"Yes, a spy is someone who dresses up like someone else to get inside of a place that they are not wanted in order to get something. And sometimes it can be really dangerous, even life-threatening. You should ask your Mamma more about that," Miss Jones explained.

"Meema told me how one of you Joneses was found…" My voice dropped.

Miss Jones's head dipped for a moment before she straightened, staring at the door as though lost in thought.

"I am sorry, Mam. I didn't mean nothing by it," I felt ashamed.

"You'd best get to lunch now, Bri," she said, her voice firmer. "It's almost over."

She rose and opened the door, waiting for me to leave. I stood and started toward the mess hall but stopped at the first step, glancing back at her. Her eyes met mine, and for a brief moment and I thought she might say something else, but she didn't. She had tears in her eyes.

"I just wanted to say, I appreciate what you've done for us," I said softly, my voice carrying a note of humility. Miss Jones paused, wiping the corners of her eyes with a delicate motion. A small smile followed, warm but laced with something deeper.

"Thank you, Bri. That's kind of you to say," she replied. "But you know how you can really prove it?"

Her words caught me off guard, and I blinked, puzzled. We both stared at each other. I looked confused.

"Prove it. Do you understand what I mean?" She asked.

"Yes, ma'am," I answered, though I wasn't entirely sure I did. Then, before she could say anything else, I blurted out, "One more thing, Miss Jones."

"What is it, Bri?" she asked, tilting her head ever so slightly.

"If you needed to know something, something someone else knows, how would you get them to tell you their secret?"

Miss Jones leaned back slightly, her hand resting on her chin as her gaze wandered off into the distance. Her thoughtful silence filled the room.

"Bri," she said finally, "you'd have to make them trust you. Trust is everything. It's hard to earn, but once it's gone, it's gone forever. You'll never get it back like you had it the first time."

Her answer wasn't what I expected, and honestly, I didn't entirely agree. I nodded anyway, but Miss Jones saw through me. I've always been cursed with a face that can't keep secrets; my eyes tend to do the talking.

"Trust, huh," I murmured, mostly to myself. "I got it." My eyes were at work and Miss Jones noticed.

"Bri, take your time." Miss Jones studied me for a moment, her lips pressed together like she had more to say.

Instead, she sighed and tiptoed back to her desk. She grabbed her lunch satchel, took out a napkin, and sat it on her lap.

At that moment, something clicked in my mind. **Trust**. If I wanted Mr. Stone to reveal what, or who, was in those coffins, I'd need to make him trust me first.

With the plan taking shape in my head, I dashed out of the schoolhouse and over to the mess hall, just in time to grab the last of the vittles. Most of the others were already turning in their dishes, but I managed to scrounge up a plate before Old Man Eddie stepped outside to ring the bell.

After lunch, the older students allowed the younger ones to head back to the schoolhouse first. As I followed, my focus had shifted. I couldn't shake the thought of those coffins, but I knew I had to take my time.

We finished the lesson for the day, and Miss Jones announced a new assignment: Each older student was to pair up with a younger one to guide them through their studies. Our first task? To help the little ones replace "da" with "th" when they spoke. "This will be a big part of your grade," Miss Jones had warned, her voice firm.

Grades.

The only thing that I hated about school.

I got paired with Suma, Pam's little sister. She loved school, which made my job a breeze. Bright for her age, she even taught me a thing or two along the way.

But my newfound partnership didn't sit well with Jholie.

Jholie didn't say much at first, but her jealousy came out in other ways. She'd hide my school supplies before my sessions with Suma. I called her out, threatening to tell Mamma. She knew that I wouldn't and kept right on meddlin'.

Some days, after a long ride, I'd find my pencils snapped in half, some so short they were barely usable. Some of them would be so bad that they would be down to the nub. The next day in class, Jholie and Micah would sit and giggle as they watched me struggle to use the miniature pencil.

They really found it funny when Miss

Jones chewed me out about the condition of my school supplies. This went on for a few weeks or so until Jholie got bored with her jokes and antics. Jholie didn't usually get bored quickly. She was the type of kid that didn't mind being alone. And me? I'd learned to let her be. Trust might take time, but I was learning to play the long game.

CHAPTER 14

The Confrontation

School was on a 7-notch break. Every
day that Mamma made her mark, I knew we
were closer to going back. I thought a lot
about what Miss Jones said about trust and
speaking like an adult. It didn't make a
lot of sense at first, but dealing with
Mamma, Bam, and Mr. Stone helped me to
understand it more.

One early morning, with my thoughts
heavy, I wandered down to the woods to
clear my head. In the distance, I spotted
Mr. Stone chopping trees. He paused mid-
swing when he saw me, then set his ax on
his shoulder and began walking my way, his
heavy boots crunching against the earth.

When he finally reached me, he was

breathing hard, his eyes sharp and unreadable. He lowered the ax, but not by much.

"Whacha want?" He barked.

"I ain't want nothing, I was just out thankin'...I mean *thinking*."

"Well, aint'cha smart nah. His ax cut the air. Get from here, girl," he sneered.

I knew he wasn't playing, but I was not afraid. He held the ax right up to my nose.

"I don't have to. This Slope and we's free," I mouthed back.

The air between us grew taut, but before either of us could speak, a piercing cry rang out from somewhere close. A child's cry.

"Now get from 'round here, I said. I'm busy and don't need no 'stractions," he snapped.

"I ain't going," I sassed.

Mr. Stone's head snapped in the direction of the sound. Without another word, he marched off, gripping the ax tighter. He didn't look back, but I followed him anyway. He knew that I'd heard it, too. The cries grew louder as we approached his carriage. When he realized I was still trailing him, he stopped and glared at me.

"Didn't I tell you to get gone?" he snapped again.

"Oh girl, nah look at what you done did," Mr. Stone mumbled.

Reaching into the carriage, he pulled out a high-yellow baby swaddled in cloth. His demeanor shifted in an instant. Gone was the gruff man wielding an ax; now, he was tender, cradling the infant close to his chest.

"There, there now," He cooed I'm here. There. There," he was calm and gentle.

My eyes almost touched my eyebrows.

Mr. Stone calmed the crying baby and placed it back into the cart.

"I knew I saw a baby that night," I said, my voice low with realization. Whose baby is this?"

"None of your biness'. I'll string you up myself if ya' tells anyone," he growled, his tone darkening again.

His words hung heavy in the air, but instead of fear, I felt a spark of determination. I immediately thought about my conversations with Miss Jones and knew this was the moment that I had been waiting for. I had to be careful and not push too soon. I couldn't resist. There was a burning in my gut.

"I ain't gonna tell," I said smoothly, leaning against a nearby tree.

"As long as you tell me what's in those coffins."

Mr. Stone began to pack up his tools.

"What coffins?" Mr. Stones walked around to the front of his wagon and mounted his horse.

"Okay. That's how you want it. I can't wait to tell Mamma," Mr. Stone threatened.

Although I dreaded the thought, I started to walk off.

Mr. Stone jumped down off his steed and marched right up to me.

"I'll tell ya, just not right nah,"

Mr. Stone wiped the sweat from his brow.

"Well, when then. I think you lying?" I challenged.

His jaw tightened, "You ain't been taught no better than that? Don't tell no grown-up theys' lying," he snapped back.

"Call it what you want," I said, folding my arms. "Lying, bending the truth, twisting it, whatever makes you feel better."

"Would you hush, fo' you wake the baby?" Mr. Stone raised his fist and looked back at the carriage.

Cries are heard from within the carriage.

"Too late," Mr. Stone walked back to the carriage and started to grab for the baby.

"Give me the baby, you don't know what you are doing." I interrupted. Truth be told, I didn't either.

"But you do?" Mr. Stone gives the baby to me.

I wrapped the baby, put him up on my shoulder, and gently patted his back. I was shocked. I've never done that before. I've only seen it done, but it worked. I couldn't let Mr. Stone know that this was my first time. I needed him to trust me.

"He likes me more than you," I said with a small laugh, masking my surprise at how easily I'd calmed him.

"Never mind that. I have to be getting' back," he scolded.

"Not till you tell me about those coffins and that tunnel," I pressed.

"Girl, I said not nah. I'll tell you later, bu'chu' betta not tell a soul 'bout this baby." Mr. Stone snatched the baby from me then he put the sleeping baby back in the carriage and mounted his horse, again.

"How long you think you going to be able to hide a whole baby?" I asked, crossing my arms.

"As long as I need to," he said, clicking his tongue to spur the horse forward.

We went our separate ways, but I kept glancing back, watching his figure grow smaller in the distance. Something told me our conversation wasn't over, not by a long shot.

CHAPTER 15

Deeply Rooted

Although Mr. Smalls loved the sea, he knew that it would be time to dock soon. That was easier said than done. Land was nowhere in sight and neither was that white woman's baby. Mrs. Smalls didn't care at all about the missing baby or the white woman left behind. She hated white women for what her mistress did to her momma.

Mrs. Smalls' story echoed that of countless others scarred by slavery, but she bore the burden with a personal bitterness. Her master, a man of little subtlety, had been infatuated with her mother, Yandi. His wife, the mistress, knew it too well. This wasn't uncommon, but the mistress's response was anything but ordinary.

The mistress despised Yandi with a venom that burned in her eyes. She was pissed that the master shared the bed of a slave more than he frequented her own. On top of that, the mistress noticed that Yandi was treated better than all of the other slaves, an unspoken privilege that set her apart. The mistress didn't understand why her husband would behave so recklessly. Nonetheless, if the master was happy so was Yandi, which produced an okay living situation for Mrs. Smalls, as a child.

One day, the master anxiously retired to his study. He looked around briefly, and only noticed, Plat standing at his usual post near the study's door. His mind was somewhere else, because he walked right past the mistress without seeing her standing in the darkness of the hallway.

"Boy go get me a Brandy," the slave master waved his hand in the air before he reached the door.

The young slave walked over to the

buffet, lifted a decanter, and poured a small glass of spirits. He walked the glass over to the slave master, being extra careful not to earn himself another beating. He didn't drip a drop on the bearskin rug that master was so proud of.

The mistress didn't make herself known to him as her eyes followed him through the doors of the study. She watched as he opened the cabinet that contained his cigar boxes. He slowly lowered all 3 boxes from the shelf.

Each box of cigars was for a different occasion. The gold box of cigars was for the celebration of a slave child being born. This box was emptiest. The brown wooden box was for the celebration of his own child being born. This box contained the most cigars. The metal box of cigars was for any new deals on land that had been acquired.

All boxes were a symbol of his economic growth but this was a secret that only he and the mistress shared. When the master pulled out the wooden box full of foreign cigars and began to light one, the mistress made her presence known to him. And in the upcoming days, when Yandi emerged from her shack, belly swollen with life, the mistress turned cold. She promised God that that baby would never take its first breath and she always kept her promises.

When the master would go away on trips, the mistress seized her opportunities. She would call for Yandi in the middle of the night and have her whipped, burned, and sometimes beaten almost to death. After Yandi lost the baby, the mistress left her alone for a while. Yandi was left alone to recover for her next beating. The mistress's wrath, however, only festered, waiting for an outlet. When the master returned, he visited Yandi daily. The mistress's rage grew. She vowed that something more had to be done.

There was one time in particular that imbued the hate that currently stains Mrs. Small's heart. While the master was away, the mistress sold her momma to the deep south, spinning a tale of attempted escape to explain her absence upon his return. She told the master that Yandi ran off with another Buck. Without anyone able to speak up on Yandi's behalf, it was done. Yandi's young daughter, the future Mrs. Smalls, was left to endure her own struggles.

Every slave knew that being sold to the deep south meant three things; you would never see your kin again, beatings were brutal, and you worked until you dropped dead. On top of the fact that she would never see her momma again, the young Mrs. Smalls knew that with her momma being gone, the mistress would start in on her soon.

It didn't help that she was the spitting image of her mother, but unlike her mother, Mrs. Smalls had the courage to escape. Mrs. Smalls wouldn't wait to suffer. She didn't think twice when she saw the young Mr. Smalls arrive on his master's ship at the edge of the river offering freedom from the plantation.

Later that day, her mistress's overseer found the washtub and linens spread all over the ground. He assumed that she killed herself because of what happened to her mother and thought nothing else of her. Her escape was covered by the plantation's whispers. Most of whom knew that the young Yan was a great swimmer and her drowning would be by choice.

CHAPTER 16

Rebel with a Cause

While Mrs. Smalls' escape was an act of desperation, Mr. Smalls' plan was one of quiet rebellion. Their journeys converged at a moment when fate offered them both a sliver of hope, his carefully plotted escape aligning with her sudden flight from oppression. They were drawn together by the unspoken understanding of what it meant to reject the lives forced upon them.

Though their circumstances differed, hers fueled by grief and survival, his by a quiet defiance born of a peculiar and dangerous origin; they shared a common determination to seize freedom, whatever the cost. Mr. Smalls's story was no less

marked by secrets. He made a plan to
escape. He was his mistress's child,
unlike other slaves who are usually the
offspring of their masters. His mistress
had a thing for slave bucks that she knew
could get her killed if it was ever
discovered. It didn't stop her, tho. She
frequently called on the likes of a
strong buck when her husband was off
handling business in town. When she
turned up with-child, she knew that she
had to keep it a secret until she
couldn't hide it anymore.

His mother concealed her pregnancy,
relying on the house slaves to enact a
gruesome charade. The birth of this secret
child was a hoax, it had to be. By the
time, the unsuspecting slave master got
wind of the mistress going into labor, the
young baby Smalls had been a month old
already. He had been given to a young
negress to raise as her own but not before
his mother had the chance to name him.

After her hidden labor, the mistress
held the child in the air and stared at
him for a spell. The child, in all of his

newness, was trying to hold his head up, but like most newborns, he was an amateur. His head went bobbing around until she cuffed him close and rubbed his back. As she handed the baby over to the young negress.

"Take real good care of my firstborn, Robert. Call'em Bobby for short," she placed the child in the young negress's arms.

With very little time to recover, the mistress had to get herself together, quick. There was no way that she could show up with a flatter stomach and no baby. She thought quickly and confided in her house slaves to keep her secret. She wouldn't have been able to pull it off without them.

On the day that she planned to go into labor, everyone but the master knew about it. The mistress, who still walked around with a ball of cotton tucked in her underclothes, fell over as if she was in pain one Sunday evening. The house slaves rushed to her side and carried her off into the birthing room. A bucket of pig's blood was already set next to the bed where the mistress was in place, panting, and screaming. Inside the bucket was a dead piglet.

To start the show, the house slaves paced back and forth and cheered the mistress on while splashing water in her face. The naïve master waited outside of the door for hours. Random house slaves would exit, wait, then enter again.

All of a sudden, sounds of sorrow filled the air. Cries and moans seeped out from under the room door. One house slave rushed through the door holding blood-soaked sheets that contained the dead piglet. The master tried to stop her and take the contents of the sheets. The mistress watched as he tried to take the bloody sheets and interjected.

"Dear," she raised her voice, "I need you."

There they sat, the Master and the Mistress, mourning the death of their first child.

Because the young Mr. Smalls was the mistress's child, he had somewhat of a good life. He didn't resent white folks like Mrs. Smalls did. It could have been because he was part one.

His only real issue with white folks was how they saw him. He wasn't white enough to sit at their tables, but he wasn't black enough for the fields. He was well aware of what his place was in society and he hated it. He yearned freedom and had a gripping urge to flee the control of white society. His hate gave birth to his love for the sea, but even seamen needed to walk on land every once in a while.

He never stopped thinking about his mother and hoped that one day their paths would cross. A dream deferred by the rules of the south that eventually dried up like a raisin in the sun.

CHAPTER 17

The Deed

Mr. Smalls rose the next morning with worry settled deep in his chest. Thoughts raced through his mind, but none weighed heavier than the thought of washing up on land with a white woman in tow, one with no baby to account for. He had some time to think, but not much, as the horizon revealed an approaching ship in slow moving waters.

Unknown ships sometimes meant trouble. Though most passed without incident, this one was different. The ship was black like it had been dipped in tar with four compartments that hid cannons. This was a ship that was no stranger to war, and like most ships, all-white crew of rough, bearded men whose faces bore the filth of the sea. The white men took notice of Smalls, his all-black crew, especially the women and dropped anchor.

"Ahoy there!" came the gravelly shout from one of the men aboard the black ship.

"We don't want no trouble," the young seaman yelled out.

"Drop anchor, boy," the man from the opposing ship barked.

"I can't do that suh, my Cap'n is sleepin' and he told me not to stop this ship till' we hit land."

Smalls stepped out onto the quarter deck just as their ship drifted past the other. His heart sank as the black ship turned abruptly, circling hard to starboard, cutting off their escape. Bobby didn't know what to do. He rushed to the door of the white woman's cabin and knocked.

"I'm not hungry," she replied curtly.

"Miss, open the doe', I need your help," his voice was urgent.

The door opened slightly, and Mr. Smalls slipped inside.

"Listen, we are all in danger. I need you to act like dis' is yo' husband's ship and he is sleepin'."

"Why should I do that when you plan to throw me overboard?" she retorted, lounging back on the cot.

"If I wanted to throw you overboard, you'd be fish food by nah," Smalls said through gritted teeth. "The way I sees it is you owe me. I saved your life," Bobby peeked out of the door.

He felt the sudden yank of his ship dropping anchor.

"I didn't ask you to do that, did I?" The white woman sassed back.

"Well, don't do it for me, do it for the chillins' on board. They would kill us all, 'cluding you. Come on, we are running out of time," Bobby hurried out of the door in hopes that the white woman was following behind him.

He made it to the middle step and saw the ship, except this time, it is much closer, on the opposite side, and the cannon doors were opened.

A long pause followed before the

woman stood, fixing Smalls with a steely gaze. "Fine. Let's get this over with."

Above deck, the tension was palpable. Bobby braced himself before he addressed the hostile white crew.

"Hey, hey, wait give him a moment, like I said, he was sleepin'." Bobby negotiated.

Bobby walked to his second and nodded to him. The second knew exactly what it meant. He walked around and gathered all of the weapons he could find and placed them strategically around the ship. Mrs.

Smalls gathered the children and remaining women in a tight circle, their whispers drowned by the rhythmic lapping of the sea. Mrs. Smalls was well aware of where the weapons were placed, when like a ghost out of the fog, up walks the white woman.

"Hey what do you want, you throwing us off track," the white woman yelled.

"Sorry, Mam, I thought those niggers had stolen that ship. Fits the description. I didn't know you was on board. Glad I was wrong," he stammered, tugging off his hat.

The crew of the black ship howled and whistled at the sight of her, but the captain barked for silence.

"Well, I am on board and my husband's sleep… and if that's all, we'll be on our way, peacefully," she lied smoothly.

"Sorry, to bother you, Mam," the seaman returned his hat to his head. The white woman looked around the ship till her eyes met Mr. Smalls. Something passed between them, unspoken and uneasy, then she disappeared below deck.

Mrs. Smalls, livid, followed her at once with Mr. Smalls not too far behind.

"What the hell do you think you are doing? Who let you out?" Mrs. Smalls snarled and followed quickly behind the white woman.

"I did," Mr. Smalls interjected.

"Oh! So you planned this?" Mrs. Smalls wheeled on him.

Mr. Smalls looked away.

"Robert Anthony Smalls don't you play silent with me," Mrs. Smalls pointed her finger in his face.

"I had to baby. We wouldn't have survived without'a," Bobby said with his hands closed together as if he was praying.

Mrs. Smalls' face darkened.

"I was only trying to help," interrupted the white woman.

"Ain't that just like a white woman. We don't need your damn help. You do enough harm just existing," Mrs. Smalls stormed out of the room, slamming the door behind her.

Alone now, Cathy smirked at Mr. Smalls. "Saved your neck, didn't I? So, what now? A thank you?"

"I just wanted to say thank'ya," Smalls said, his tone cautious.

"Thank me for what?" The white woman questioned.

"Saving us. My name is Bobby, but you can call me Mr. Smalls. I'm the captain of this here ship."

"And...your master's bastard. You almost as white as me," the white woman smirked. "My name is Cathy. And I didn't do it just for you. I did it for everybody."

"Well thanks anyway. And…your wrong ya' know," Mr. Smalls added.

"About what?" Cathy asked.

"I ain't my master's bastard, I'm my mistress's," Mr. Smalls said as he closed the door.

Cathy looked sharply at Mr. Small's with awe in her eye and her mouth opened. She couldn't help but think about the baby she left behind. A tear fell from her eye that she quickly wiped before Bobby noticed it.

"Get some sleep, breakfast is early," Mr. Smalls said.

"Can you bring it to me?" Cathy said quickly. "I mean instead of your wife. She spits in my food."

"But you trust me, huh?" Mr. Stone reached for the door.

"I didn't say that either. I just think we are even. That's all." Cathy remarked.

"Even? Ain't no slave ever been even with a white woman," smirked Bobby.

"I don't see any slaves on this ship," Cathy said proudly.

"Yeah, I guess we's even," Mr. Smalls left the room.

As he closed the door, he paused just outside, listening to the faint sound of Cathy's sobs. Her sadness reminded him of a sorrow he thought buried long ago, stirring something reluctant within him.

He started to turn back, but Mrs. Smalls' glare in his mind stopped him cold. Silently, he walked away as the ship sailed onward, cradled by the moonlit sea.

CHAPTER 18

Bam & Linc

That night all I could think about was Mr. Stone and that baby. I wanted to tell Meema so bad, but I wanted Mr. Stone to trust me more. The only person that I could ever talk to about it would be Brik. I suspected that he is the only other person that knows about it besides me. I kept staring at the wall, tossing and turning all night.

Suddenly, Mamma burst through the door. I immediately played like I was asleep.

"I know you ain't sleepin'. Get up. Now." Her voice cut through the night like a blade. "We gots to hurry. Put your clothes on. It's time."

I rolled over and looked at Mamma. I
rolled back over, groggy but curious.

"Time for what?"

"Bam's baby is coming and she wants
you there," Mamma explained.

"I don't want to hear all of that
screaming and huffing and seeing all that
blood." I relented.

I rolled back onto my bed and threw
the covers over my whole body when in the
next breath, I felt them being snatched
off.

"This ain't a debate. Nah com'on we
ain't got much time. And when you seen a
baby be born before?" She ordered and
questioned in one breath.

"I ain't. Jus' heard about it is
all," I mumbled.

Mamma threw a dress over the top of
my head and yanked my arm out of the door.
From the porch, I could already hear Bam's
wails echoing through the still night air.
I froze, fear prickling my skin. I tried
to turn back around.

"Mamma, I don't want to go," I said.

"Oh, so you scared nah, huh? I ain't neva known you to be scared of nuthin', not even me."

Boy, was she wrong. The truth is, I did fear my mother just not behind her back. It's easier to get away with things when your Mamma and Deddy ain't around.

"I ain't scared…I," I lied. "I jus' don't want to see her in no pain." I tried to play it off.

Mamma shot me a sharp look.

"Well ain't that a caution. Every time you needed her she was there for you, right?" Mamma snapped back.

"Yes."

"And every time she needs you, you were there for her, weren't you?" Mamma interrogated me.

"Well, she needs you now. Let's go!" Mamma wasn't asking, and I didn't argue.

We made our way to Bam's house. As we got closer to her door, "Oh my gosh, we are too late, baby is already crying," Mamma turned and looked at me.

"Oh, Lord, we too late!" she

209

exclaimed. "Baby's already cryin'."

Mamma rushed through Bam's door and there Bam was panting, sweating, and crying all in the same breath. I walked right up to her and grabbed her hand.

"Is that a dress?" Bam noticed right away. "Where you been? You always coming late," Bam rasped.

"Don't worry about that, where is the baby?" I asked.

"It ain't c-c-ca-came out yet," Bam panted.

"Then who was that crying?" I asked. I scanned the room to find Cousin Sherry in the corner weeping her heart out. My heart thudded in my chest.

"Bam you about to have a baby," I finally accepted the inevitable.

"I know tha-" Bam was exhausted.

Bam looked at me and squeezed my hand as she let out the most agonizing scream.

"Ahhhhh!"

Linc was outside the house pacing back and forth and with every scream, he picked up the pace. Momo kneeled down in front of Bam and looked under the sheet.

"It's time," Momo announced, kneeling at the foot of the bed. "I see the head.

Okay, Bam now push with everything in you."

Bam looked at me and let out a scream that shooked the walls. Momo worked quickly. A blood-soaked baby boy emerged in her hands, his cries piercing the air. He was covered in fluid with his hair matted to his head. Bam was silent for a moment. Momo handed the moist baby to Bam and guided Bam to rest him on her nipple.

Mamma fetched Linc from outside. He walked in dripping with sweat as if he had just given birth, too. Momo pushed down on Bam's stomach and Bam started screaming again, a sound so raw it made my stomach churn.

"Mamma, what's happening?" I whispered, dread creeping in.

Momo looked under the sheet and saw the legs of an infant. She looked at Cousin Sherry with worry on her face.

"There is another one coming but it's feet first," Momo said.

The room stilled.

A loud thud is heard. Linc hit the floor face first. He was out cold. Ms. Betty, Cousin Sherry's best friend, and Bam's Momma grabbed a pillow and stuffed it under Linc's head. Mamma took the baby from Bam and put him right in my arms.

"What you want me to do with it?" I stared at the moist child for a spell. He kind of looked like Bam but he wore Linc's nose. He looked back at me and stopped crying.

"You hold him," Mamma barked, rushing back to Bam's side.

Bam started crying.

"Now Bam, I need you to get yourself together. You in for a fight. Are you ready?" Momo questioned.

Bam, exhausted with fear, raised her head and looked at Momo square in the eye.

"I ain't got nothin' left in me," Bam said restlessly. Bam was pale, her head lolling. "I can't," she whimpered, her voice barely audible.

"Yes, you do chile. You can do this. Plenty babies come into the world like this," Momo shot back. "You

212

somebody's mamma now. Act like it."

"But I'm so tired." Bam dropped her head with exhaustion. Tears streamed down Bam's face, but she nodded weakly, summoning strength from somewhere deep.

"Cousin Sherry, go grab some mo' clean towels. Betty, we don't have much time." Momo rushed. "She is losing a lot of blood. I'm gon' have to go in and turn it round'."

By this time, Ms. Betty filled a pail with cool water. She raised the pail and turned it upside down on Linc. He jumped up wiping the water out of his face and nose. Ms. Betty left and returned with the towels. Momo placed the towels on the floor between Bam's legs. They turned bright red instantly.

"Nah Bam, look at me girl," Momo encouraged Bam. She raised her head with tears running down her face. She reached her hand out for mine then dropped it. Her head dropped and her eyes closed shut.

"Oh my God!" Ms. Betty cried.

Momo reached inside of Bam from under the sheet and fiddled. Minutes dragged

213

like hours. Momo emerged with a baby girl in hand. They gave the baby to Linc who cuffed her like one of his balls.

"We gotta stop the bleeding after I pull this sac out," Momo added.

Blood soaked the towels at an alarming rate. Momo pushed Bam's stomach and a red and gray colored sac spilled to the floor. It looked like a huge blood clot. Momo quickly stuffed Bam with towels.

"Let's move her into the other bed, she gon' need a lot of rest to pull through this."

"What you mean, stop the bleeding?" Linc demanded, panic in his voice.

"She's lost a lot of blood and some don't make it. But look at those beautiful healthy babies. Let's let her rest and focus on those babies. We have to get them cleaned up and fed."

"No, not my baby," cried Ms. Betty.

Linc handed the baby to his momma, walked over to Bam, grabbed a pillow from her side, and wiped the sweat from her brow. He knelt beside Bam and placed the

pillow on the floor, his hand trembling as
he brushed her damp hair back.

"You hear me, Bam? You gon' be okay.

We got two beautiful babies. Stay
with me, girl."

"What you think you doing, boy?"
questioned Cousin Sherry.

"Xcuse' me, I am man nah. I'm
somebody's Daddy. And we made those babies
together and we gon' see'em together and
not a moment sooner," demanded Linc.

The room was heavy with tension, but
in that moment, the cries of the newborns
filled the silence, a fragile reminder of
life, even in the shadow of uncertainty.

I found myself marveling at Linc
again. His dedication to Bam was
unwavering. He refused to leave her side,
his love for her plain in every gesture.

The babies were being tended to by
the women of Slope, but Linc's sole focus
was Bam. It was clear: she was his world.
At that moment, I knew he loved her more
deeply than words could convey.

Mamma took the baby girl whose eyes
were wide opened, she had not yet cried

215

and wiped her clean. She swaddled the infant in a soft blanket Meema had sewn, a gift for Bam and Linc's firstborn. There was only one problem, no one had planned for two babies.

They had one of everything that a new Momma needed but now, they needed two of everything. The ladies of Slope, under the direction of Cousin Sherry, began work on making materials as soon as they heard. In the meantime, Bam's Momma took the boy child and wrapped him in a blanket given to her by Mr. Stone.

Days had passed and Bam didn't move.

Linc and I started to lose hope when we heard she got the fever. I was surprised he didn't get sick, too. He wasn't eating right and he only left her side to relieve himself. He helped wash her every day and he even threw out her soiled towels when it was time.

It was like Bam had transformed Linc in some way. Meema always said that a man never knows who he truly is until he finds the right woman. One evening, I visited Bam, Linc was brushing her hair and talking to her. This was a side that I'd never seen in him, either.

Mamma and Deddy visited Linc everyday.

"Look at that boy," Deddy was impressed.

"Remind you of somebody?" Mamma teased.

"Maybe a little," Deddy resolved.

"Maybe a lot… Meema told me how you didn't leave my side either," Mamma batted her eyes.

Deddy blushed, "That woman is getting old, don't believe everything you hear. I'll leave the babysitting to the women folk."

"Hey, boy," Deddy got Linc's attention. "You keep doing what you doing. It works everytime," Deddy smiled at Mamma, leaving her with a kiss on the cheek.

Linc nodded to Deddy then refocused his attention to Bam.

"I miss you like crazy, please wake up. I promise to build you a great big house like you want and maybe a boat, too.

I know how you like to be out on the
water. I already started collecting the
wood. Old Mr. Stone being super nice, too.
He gave me a bunch of logs to use and a
blanket for our baby boy. I can't wait for
us to see'em and be a family. Come back to
me Bam," Linc rested his head on her side.
"God send me a sign that this is gonna be
okay. I'm a good boy…I mean man. I'll do
right by them all."

Thunder rumbled overhead, a low
warning or a sign. The sky darkened, and
rain began to pour, heavy and relentless.
I mounted Hadie and rode hard through the
storm, my heart pounding.

Linc opened the looking hole to see
what was happening. He loved the smell of
the air when it rained. The storm had a
strange energy to it, like something was
shifting. He stared out of the hole for a
while when he heard a raspy voice.

"Linc, I want a drink of water, not a
rain bath. Close that hole," Bam sassed.

Linc froze. He turned slowly,
disbelief etched across his face. It was

Bam. Awake. Talking. Sassing him like nothing had happened. He turned around in amazement and dropped to the floor.

He dropped to his knees beside her, kissed her lips, then bolted for the door. He ran to the door and yelled for his Mamma.

"Mamma, Mamma, Mamma!" Linc called.

Cousin Sherry opened their door which was just across the way. She stumbled down the steps. On her way over she yelled for Ms. Betty who was in the prayer house.

"Boy, you know I got these babies to tend to," Cousin Sherry said.

"She's awake, Mamma! Bam's awake!" Linc shouted, his voice cracking.

"Oh, thank God!" Cousin Sherry ran back into the house to tell the other ladies. Bam's Mamma came shooting out of the door.

"Boobie, go get Bri! Tell her Bam is wake!" Ms. Betty shouted. A huge crowd started to gather outside of Bam's house.

Soon as I heard, I rode Hadie right up to her porch, hopped down, and forced my way past everyone. My eyes were full of tears, but I wiped them away before Bam could see.

"Bout time! You had us all worried!" I blurted, tears threatening to spill.

"I can tell you been crying," Bam said.

"I can tell you need to lick your lips," I cracked. Bam giggled then licked her lips.

Cousin Sherry brought the babies for Bam to hold.

"I thought it was just a dream. We got two babies for real, tho?" she whispered.

Bam fell back with her eyes closed still clutching the babies. Everyone, except me, panicked. She rose with a smile.

"Gotcha!" Bam cracked.

Laughter rippled through the house. Even Bam joined in, though it left her breathless. She turned to Linc.

"See what we made? What did you name them?" Bam questioned.

Linc looked sheepish, "I didn't. I

was waiting on you."

"You mean to tell me that you didn't name our babies. How long have I been asleep?" Bam asked.

"Three days straight," I said. "Oh well, we still got time," Bam added.

"What are you talking about?" Linc asked.

"Old Sara said it's bad luck not to name a baby within the first three days. We almost missed it," Bam remarked.

"Well, Linc, what you think?" asked Bam.

"How about you name the girl and I'll name the boy," Linc suggested.

"Okay. I'll go first. Jessie is a fine name, but we gon' call her Jess," Bam said with a tired but radiant smile.

"Okay. This here boy," Linc said proudly, "is gon' be called Rufus, after my Daddy."

Cousin Sherry wiped away tears as the room filled with warmth.

That night, after the storm finished raging, I walked to the edge of the woods where I found myself in a position that I had never experienced before. I was on my knees looking up at the night sky. I figured if it had worked for Linc it had to work for me.

"Well, I ain't never done nothin' like this before," I muttered, feeling small against the heavens. "But thank you for Bam and them babies. Look out for my Meema, please. She ain't tellin' no one, but I know she ain't doin' too good. I love her and want her to stick around."

As if in response, thunder boomed, shaking the ground. Without warning, the sky lit up and the brightest lightning bolt came flashing down. It connected with a tree not too far from me, splitting it in two and sending me to my knees. The tree caught fire but the fire was quickly dissolved by the rain. Was the Creator talking back to me? If this was a sign, it couldn't be good. Someone or something in Slope was in danger.

CHAPTER 19

The Truth

Land was not too far off in the distance, the morning sun casting an amber haze over the horizon. Mr. Smalls was on deck alone, his hands resting on the ship's worn railing. The sea whispered against the hull, and the salty breeze did little to soothe the tightness in his chest. Behind him, quiet footsteps approached, and he turned just as Mrs. Smalls handed him a steaming cup of coffee.

"Mornin', you up early," she remarked, standing close beside him. "There's got to be worry on yo' mind," she went on.

"Yeah, there is," he admitted, gazing

out at the expanse of ocean. Mrs. Smalls looked at him knowingly.

"Go on, tell me 'bout it," she insisted.

He exhaled.

"You know we need to dock soon. We runnin' mighty low on supplies. I jus…" shrugged Mr. Smalls.

"You don't know how a bunch of niggas, gone dock on white shores with a white woman aboard. We can't." Mrs. Smalls interrupted. "Throw her over, she evil."

Mrs. Smalls hugged Mr. Smalls from the back and squeezed him a little.

"We'll be fine. We've done it befoe' just not with a white woman on board. Everyone on board knew what to do."

He frowned, still unconvinced. "I know babe, but what if something goes wrong? We'd all sho' be strung up on a tree if anyone found out. Can't you feel it, the way it's hangin' over us like a storm?" Mr. Smalls stood aside.

She squeezed him briefly and stepped back, "Nothing will go wrong. You stop worrying nah, I got to get breakfast started," Mrs. Smalls walked off. She left him standing there as her dress swept below deck. But as Mrs. Smalls reached the narrow hallway near the white woman's cabin, she paused. Pressing an ear against the wooden door, she listened for movement, then rapped sharply with her knuckles. The door opened slowly. The knock carried the authority of familiarity, and a moment later, the door creaked open.

"I don't want breakfast," Cathy said before Mrs. Smalls could speak.

"I wasn't bringing you no breakfast.

I gots' something to say," Mrs. Smalls stepped inside without waiting for an invitation.

Cathy opened the door completely. Mrs. Smalls walked in and immediately covered her nose. The room reeked of fish and sweat.

"Damn, you need a bath. How you breathin' in here?" Mrs. Smalls smirked.

"What do you want?" Cathy asked tersely, glaring at her.

"Listen, we bout to dock soon and

don't need no trouble out'a ya'. If you is good, we might set you free since Bobby is so dead set on not throwing yo' smelly body overboard." Her words sliced sharp, and then, with a warning tilt of her head, she added, "But don't test me. I might solve this problem myself if you step outta line."

"Is that all?" Cathy walked over to the door and placed her hand on the spine. She turned to leave but not before delivering a stinging slap when Cathy muttered under her breath. The sound cracked against the tense air.

"Watch your mouth, white bitch. On this ship, you ain't nobody special," Mrs. Smalls walked away.

Cathy shut the door with a trembling hand once Mrs. Smalls was gone. Dropping onto the rough cot, her mind filled with fractured thoughts, thoughts of Slope, her baby, her regrets. Silent tears streaked her cheeks. For all her defiance, this ship was a prison just as much as Slope had been. The only tether to her resolve was the idea that she could, somehow, make it back to her son.

Being held captive in Slope was much better than being slapped every day on this dirty ship. At least I would have my son, she thought. She knew that there had to be some way for her to get back to him and planning an escape when they docked could be her only opportunity.

Moments later, there was another knock at her door. By the sound of it, she knew who it was. It wasn't the angry knock she had grown accustomed to, but it was a friendlier sound.

"Breakfast," Mr. Smalls said gently.

Cathy opened the door. She was happy to see him. She knew that she could reason with him but she didn't want to bring it up in front of Mrs. Smalls.

"I'm ready to tell you," Cathy stated.

Mr. Smalls stepped inside cautiously. "Tell me what?"

"Where my baby is," Cathy whispered.

Mr. Smalls froze. He closed the door and lowered himself onto a stool near Cathy. She slightly moved away but not too

227

far. She knew she smelled and that made her uncomfortable.

Cathy's voice faltered.

"I ain't no baby killer. I left my baby back at that place with all those free Coloreds…with his Daddy," Cathy revealed.

Mr. Smalls' mouth hung open from surprise. He was speechless but mustered up a few words.

"See that's where you wrong. Niggas on this land ain't never been free. That piece of paper the white man give you don't mean nothing. I done seen a freeman get his paper ripped up right in front of him," Mr. Smalls flung his hands in the air. "What you telling me all dis fo'?"

"Ain't no white men back at that place. They don't need a paper there," Cathy pleaded. "I want you to take me back there. To get my boy, he is special," said Cathy.

Mr. Smalls stood up. "Wait, wait, we can't go back there. You know what they do to folks like you. They'd kill you fo' sho' this time and by the way, I'se supposed to done that fo'em. That's why you on dis' here ship or have you forgotten," Mr. Smalls stood abruptly.

"But you didn't," Cathy shot back, standing now. "You spared me, so you owe me!"

"Nah, we's even, remember." Mr. Smalls replied.

"Okay then, we's even and I'll owe you one," Cathy added.

"You know my Misses won't have it," Mr. Smalls got serious.

Cathy dropped to the floor and tugged at Mr. Smalls' britches. Mr. Smalls covered his nose.

"Please, just consider it. If not, throw me over now. I have no reason to live," Cathy pleaded.

Mr. Smalls grabbed Cathy by the shoulders and brought her to her feet. She wiped her nose and stood tall. Mr. Smalls saw sympathy in her eyes and understood the feeling of being ripped away from family. He couldn't help but to remember the feeling, however, he snatched away in anger.

"Nah you see how we been feeling all this time. You sell our babies, sistas, brothas, daddies, and sometimes Mommas. We never see'em again. Don't know if they's dead or 'live but nah you feel it, too."

Mr. Smalls stumped out of the door.

Cathy rushed after him and grabbed his arm.

"I know, but I'm not like them," said Cathy.

"Nah, but you look like 'em," Mr. Smalls replied.

"Think about your own mama, what she went through to keep you safe. You of all people should understand this. You just like my son," Cathy pressed.

Mr. Smalls stopped and stared at the door. Her words struck something deep within him, and for a fleeting moment, she saw the conflict in his eyes. The thought of his Momma's struggles to keep him safe, passed through his mind. He turned, walked away, and disappeared above deck. On his way up, he noticed that by nightfall they will be close to land and will have to dock. He thought about what Cathy said and

what going back to Slope could mean for
her. He knew exactly how she felt on both
ends, but facing Mrs. Smalls could feel
much worse. He knew he didn't have to and
the risk he'd be taking if he did.

Cathy sagged against the wall, tears
brimming again, as outside, the sea
carried the ship steadily closer to land
and the uncertain dangers it promised.

CHAPTER 20

The Vision

Today was our last lesson with Miss. Jones for this part of the school season. Miss Jones finished this season with a story about death. She directed us to meet in the big circle, next to the schoolhouse. She carried a small wooden box with her.

We were all seated.

The detail on the box caught my eye immediately. The faded carvings and scratches seemed to whisper untold secrets. As we settled, Miss Jones raised a finger to her lips, calling for silence. We obeyed, and the circle fell quiet, except for the occasional rustle of the wind through the grass.

With deliberate care, she lifted the

lid of the box. Our eyes were glued on her
movements. She raised the lid from the box
to reveal a glass case. Within the case
was a spider, a vivid creature with a
shimmering body almost the size of my
palm. It tapped against the glass as
though it shared our curiosity. Miss
Jones placed the case gently on the
ground in the center of the circle.

"This is Anansi, the Spider God. He
wanted me to tell you about his run-in
with Brother Death."

At that moment, the spider began
clawing at the glass. The younger children
edged forward, craning for a better look,
but Miss Jones waved us all back to our
seated positions.

"Stay on your bottoms," she said
firmly.

We obeyed, still riveted by the
restless creature inside the case.

"One day while out walking, Anansi
the spider came across a house with an old
man sitting at the entrance. The man was
so thin and frail, he looked like a pile
of skin and bones. Anansi asked the man if

he could have some water, but the man didn't respond. Being the charming trickster he was, Anansi took his lack of an answer as an enthusiastic "Yes," and proceeded to enter the house, drinking water and eating the delicious food inside.

The spider returned to eat at the house every day for seven sunsets. One evening, Anansi offered the old man his eldest daughter as a wife so that she could cook meals for Anansi whenever he visited. The old man said nothing, but when Anansi returned to the house the next morning, he found that the old man had eaten his daughter.

Anansi grew angry.

He asked the old man who he was. The man finally spoke. He told Anansi that he, too, had a secret. The old man told Anansi that he was "Brother Death" and asked Anansi why he came looking for him. He also told Anansi that he had unwittingly invited himself and his family into Brother Death's home. Anansi became frightened. He raced home to warn his family. With his burlap sack on his back, Brother Death chased Anansi through the village and into Anansi's home. The spider told his family to spin their webs and climb onto the ceiling to avoid Brother Death.

Brother Death sat on the floor, waiting for the spider family to drop. One-by-one, each member of Anansi's family lost its grip on the ceiling and fell into Death's burlap sack. Anansi was the last one holding onto the ceiling when he told Brother Death that he was so full from eating his food that his body would shatter if he fell to the floor.

Brother Death pondered on the idea that if Anansi fell, he would get nothing. Since Brother Death wanted to eat Anansi, he agreed to let Anansi lower himself. Anansi told Brother Death to put a barrel of flour under him to break his fall, but when Death did this, Anansi jumped on his head and pushed Brother Death's face into the flour. The flour bath temporarily blinded Brother Death.

Anansi jumped off Brother Death's

head, released his family and they ran for their lives. Brother Death has never caught Anansi the Spider. That is why I can tell you the story of Anansi on this day. Remember, when you see spider webs on the ceiling, they belong to Anansi. He is still trying to get away from Death. Now here me good, I have outsmarted Anansi by offering him protection from death."

Miss Jones removed the glass. The younger kids moved away in fear. Shockingly, the spider didn't run away. Instead, it moved around in a circle, surveying the area, as if he was looking for Brother Death. Miss Jones returned the glass cover to the case where the spider sat waiting for its protection.

She looked out into the crowd, "What did you learn from the tale of Anansi and Brother Death?"

Hands shot into the air, eager for her attention. There wasn't an arm not raised. She pointed to Brik, who stood first.

"I think the story is telling us that death is coming for us all and he won't stop chasing us, so we should live and fall in love before it's too late," Brik looked at me.

I looked away.

"Right, Brik," Miss Jones beckoned for him to sit. "And, anyone else?"

Fewer hands shot in the air. Miss Jones selected Gene.

He stood.

"I think the story is telling us to watch what we do because our actions could put others in danger," Gene looked at me.

I frowned.

"Good insight, Gene," Miss Jones said, motioning for him to take his seat. "And anyone else?"

The circle fell quiet. My hand was the only one left in the air. Miss Jones met my gaze.

"Yes, Bri?"

I stood slowly, the weight of all eyes upon me.

"I think the story is telling us to not go looking for Brother Death because we just might find him," I said, my voice steady but quiet.

"Yes, Bri. You, too, are right," Miss Jones motioned for me to sit down.

"One last thing, you have all been good students and if it is in the Creator's plan, I'll see some of you next season. Good day!" She exhaled deeply, the weight of her words sinking into the silence.

I walked away from the doors of the schoolhouse feeling both empty and enlightened. There was so much more I needed to know, on top of the scattered truths I had already gathered. I'm not just talking about school stuff either. Slope was riddled with secrets, and I wanted to uncover every last one. With only one session of school left, I was determined to learn enough to begin my journey and peel back the mysteries of the world beyond this town.

Later that day, I went to visit Lilly on the way to Bam's house. As I got closer to Lilly's house, I could see Lilly's Nana, sitting still on the porch, gray eyes, long white hair flowing like a cloud against her deep brown skin. Lilly talked of how her Nana would sleep with her eyes opened and I didn't know if this was one of those times.

I crept toward the door, cautious, when a low, gravelly voice stopped me cold.

"Your Meema ain't taught you no betta' dan' dat' girl?"

"Yes, mam. I though--t"

"Thought what?" she snapped, her tone sharp as a knife. "You betta watch yo'self, girl. I had me a dream a little while ago. Saw you walkin' on water in the middle of the river. Then you fell straight down to the bottom. And I ain't seen you come up yet," she began to rock, the creak of her chair keeping time with her words. "What have you gotten yourself into, girl?" she asked, her voice rising into a screech.

I backed away, my heart hammering in my chest. My lips refused to form words, so I simply moved, down the steps, keeping my eyes locked on hers.

"You don't want to tell me huh? Well, whateva' it is, it's gon' be hard for you to get out," her laughter, sharp and chilling, echoed in my ears. "I ain't seen you come up yet, haha, I ain't seen you come up yet, ahahaa."

I ran all the way to Bam's house, without looking back. When I got there, I didn't even knock on the door. My palms were sweating and my legs were shaking. I walked to the side of Bam's house and sat down, out of sight.

That old woman doesn't know what she's talking about, I told myself. She didn't see me walking on water, but what if she did? What does it mean? Am I in trouble?

I heard an ax swinging in the distance. I tried to lift myself up, but my legs were still wobbly. Somehow, I made it to my feet. I walked around to the front of Bam's house to find Brik chopping wood. I'd hope he didn't see me but he did. He gestured for me to come over. I pulled myself together and walked over to him.

"You alright?" he said curiously.

"Yeah, I'm good. What's going on?" I

replied, still shaking. He stopped chopping.

"My Daddy told me you know," he looked at me.

"Know what?" I tried to play it off.

"Oh, so that's how you gonna act. Well, okay. I'll go along with this," he agreed.

The burn to speak clawed at me, but I bit it back. I wanted Mr. Stone to trust me more. What if Brik was bluffing just to see if I'd talk so that he could go back and tell his Daddy? And if his daddy was testing me, this wasn't the time to slip. I had to play it safe, but what if Brik knew about the secrets of the gate and beneath the schoolhouse? He could definitely shed some light on one of Slope's secrets for me.

I could tell that Brik was sweet on me, but I had no interest in him. He was regular in every sense of the word, someone that Mamma expected me to marry.

"I wrote something for you," he smiled.

"Yeah, let me hear it," I said,

feigning interest.

"No, this ain't the right time," he replied with a grin.

"Well, why did you mention it, then?" I asked.

"I just wanted to see if you wanted to hear it," he said.

"Bye, Brik." I turned and walked away, shaking my head as he called after me.

I turned and started walking back down the strip towards my house.

"One day, it will be the perfect time," he yelled.

I kept walking. On the way, I stopped by the mess hall just to gather my thoughts, hoping no one was there. Lilly's Nana's haunting laugh was still echoing in my mind. I opened the door of the hall and found Sara sitting all alone at the head of the horseshoe table, her usual brooding presence almost tangible. She gave me a look, a sharp glare meant to send kids scattering, but she didn't know me well because if she did she would have known, no look could scare me off. I've had a lot of practice.

"Oh, so you different?" Sara finally said, her voice dripping with sarcasm.

I was shocked because I'd never heard her say a word, not even at the festival. I didn't say a word. I sat down at the end of the horseshoe. She pulled a flask from underneath the table and took a long swig then slammed it down on the table.

"Why you hear girl?" she questioned.

I didn't answer.

"You won't win this battle. I can keep quiet longer than you." Sara smirked.

But she was wrong. Her words reminded me of something, a suspicion that maybe Sara wasn't just guarding secrets but was shaped by them too. My mind came to me.

Sara can keep a secret. She could also help with a secret. I got up from the end of the horseshoe and walked along the horseshoe, keeping my eyes on her. I sat down right next to her.

"Why you always sad, Miss Sara?" I asked gently.

"Who said I was sad?" She shot back.

"No one, you just look it," I

243

responded.

Her expression shifted, her eyes falling to the table. A single tear dropped onto the wood, and she quickly wiped it away.

"Where your family at? Why are you here alone?" I questioned.

She dropped her head, like usual but quickly raised it.

"You ask too many questions. I'm leaving," she raised the flask once again then exhaled a long sigh.

"Wait, Miss Sara, don't go. I need to know," I continued. "Will you tell me?"

Sara flopped back down.

"I had a family, once…a man and two babies," Sara reminisced.

"What happened to them?" I questioned.

"You ask…" Sara started to speak.

"Please Miss Sara," I interrupted.

Her shoulders trembled as she answered, "One of my sweet babies… he died."

Her voice broke, and I wrapped an arm around her, resting my head on her shoulder. She stiffened at first, unaccustomed to comfort, but softened in the embrace. I could tell that she was not used to this kind of affection. She became soft.

"What if I could get you a new baby? Would you like that?" I asked.

Sara's eyes grew bright, but quickly dimmed, "What are you saying girl. One of your little friends in trouble, again?" Sara responded.

"No, not one of my friends. Just someone I know. He could use your help hiding a secret," I explained.

"Ha, what you know about secrets? This place is crawling wit'em. And now I guess you are adding your own," Sara teased.

At that moment, I realized that Sara was right. Not only was I a part of Slope, but I was a part of its secrets, too. I knew of a secret, and now I was creating my own. It still didn't stop me from thinking that this could be a way to earn Mr. Stone's trust. That baby is going to need a Momma and Sara is the perfect fit to pull this off, but I have got to move quickly. We sat there discussing our next moves.

CHAPTER 21

The Surprise

I started whispering in Sara's ear just in case anyone else was in the mess hall when all of a sudden, Jholie burst through the door.

"I've been looking all over for you. It's Meema. Hurry come quick," Jholie said.

My heart jumped as I vaulted over the table and bolted past her, thoughts racing with what could have gone wrong. I began to run across the strip when I noticed that it was heavily lit and everyone was outside.

"Surprise," they all screamed.

Mamma stood in the center of the crowd holding a cake that was lit with candles. Her smile stretched wide as she beckoned me forward. I looked around the crowd and saw everyone there.

"I wanted to surprise you. You are in your fifteenth year," Mamma said.

Deddy brought Hadie around, she was wearing a brand new saddle with my name on it. Deddy raised her hooves to find my name on the bottom. They used to say Thompson Plantation on the bottom but now they were custom fit.

Bam walked up to me and handed me an awkward dress. She claimed she just started learning how to sew and I could tell. I hugged her anyway. Gene and Paul started to beat the drums and Brik stepped forward.

"It's the perfect time." Brik bowed to the crowd.

He walked right up in front of me and everyone got quiet. I'd hoped that he wasn't about to get down on one knee. The Creator knows that I am not ready for that. My mind kept saying don't get down on one knee, don't get down on one knee. And to my surprise, he didn't get down on one knee. Instead, he started to speak.

"You're my strength and my spark,
The reason I strive, even in the dark. Every
step I take, every move I make,
It's all for the chance your heart should
take. You've made me better than I knew how to
be,
I just want to be someone worthy of we.
I just want to be worthy of Bri."

The words were unexpected, simple yet poignant, and I felt a faint blush rising to my cheeks. He knelt down on one knee and held up a wooden box.

Why did he have to kneel?

Now don't get me wrong, Brik wasn't hard on the eyes, but I wasn't ready for what he wanted from me. I looked at Mamma. She was giving me that look that said, "Take that box and smile about it."

My mind raced. Don't be a ring. Anything but a ring. I took the box. I opened it. Inside was a beautifully carved wooden whistle that was set on the end of a rope.

"Anytime you need me, just blow," he felt proud, but I could hear Linc and Paul snickering in the background. I felt relieved and impressed. I took the whistle out of the box and gave it a hard blow.

Brik stood up and puckered his lips for a kiss. I leaned forward. I could hear Jholie making nasty sounds in the background. I squeezed him real tight and planted one on his cheek.

"Thank you," I said, sincerely. "It's beautiful."

The drums picked up again, and the younger folk danced as the elders watched with soft smiles. Linc couldn't resist teasing Brik about the almost kiss.

"Come on, Brik. Pucker up again, I'll blow you a kiss this time!" he joked, shoving Brik playfully.

"Leave me alone, man. I ain't done yet. I just got to think of a way to her heart," Brik eyed me hard.

When the drums stopped the party was over. We all chipped in on the cleaning.

As the night wore on and folks began to wander home, Sara pulled me aside.

"We're not finished talking," she whispered.

"I know," I whispered back.

"I'll do the impossible by going along with your little plan, but if I do, you gotta do the impossible for me, too," Sara explained.

"And what is that?" I asked warily.

"Give that Brik boy a chance at your heart," Sara said.

I blinked, taken back, "Why do you care?" I asked.

"I don't, but you ain't getting no younger. Fifteenth year, huh? Ooh, you better hurry up before he eyes someone else. Look at the way the other girls look at him. He's a handsome fella you know," Sara remarked.

I turned and saw Brik surrounded by a group of girls not that much younger than me. I don't know what came over me, but I felt a little jealous and it showed on my face and the look in my eye.

Sara noticed it, too.

"I thought you didn't care?" she quipped.

"I don't," I snapped, turning away before I betrayed myself further.

"Then why are your eyebrows about to

touch your scalp?" Sara teased. "Uh-huh. Sure," Sara's laughter echoed softly as we parted.

Did the spirit of my Mamma jump into me? Couldn't be, but maybe it did. I wasn't ashamed. I started to march over there and slap him on the back of his neck but I didn't. I held myself together.

"We'll talk later," Sara said.

"Yeah, later," I agreed.

By this time, everyone started to leave. The sound of doors shutting reverberated through the strips.

Back at home, everyone was settling down in their rooms when I heard Meema struggling through a coughing spell, calling for me. I went to her. She was sitting on her bed. On top of her covers sat a neatly wrapped box with a big white bow.

"I saved this one for last. Your Mamma wanted to give it to you but she just didn't know how," Meema explained.

I walked over and sat on the edge of Meema's bed. I tugged at the bow and it easily fell open. I took the top off and slowly peeked inside. It was a dress made from a material that I'd never seen.

"Your Mamma wore it when she married your Deddy and she was hoping that you would wear it one day," Meema said.

I looked at Meema with tears in my eyes.

"We pulled this silk and lace from one of those ships that I was telling you about and made this dress from it."

A tear fell down the side of my cheek. I tried to wipe it away before she noticed it, but she saw me.

"What's wrong, Bri?" Meema questioned.

"Meema, I don't want to get married and I don't want to have no babies," I cried.

"Oh, come on, nah. I use to feel just like you, but you getting older. And your feelings might change. Just be opened to it is all. You can't spend the rest of your life riding horses and chasing boys. They do become men, you know," Meema explained.

"Ok, Meema. I'll try," I stopped

crying.

"I'll hang this up for you and give it back to you in the morning," Meema added.

I hugged Meema and walked out of her room and into mine.

Later, in my room, I spotted the wooden box Brik had given me, now sitting at the center of my bed. Jholie pretended to read her lessons, but the glint in her eye gave her away.

"Mm-hmm," she drawled. "How did that get there?"

"Really?" I shot her a look.

I walked over to my bed, glanced at Jholie, then opened the box.

Inside was a metal key on a rope with a note tied to it. I read the note, it was from Jholie.

"Whose key did you steal?" I accused.

"I didn't steal it, just borrowed it!" Jholie responded.

"What is this a key to?" I was intrigued.

"What do you think?" Jholie said

sarcastically.

I thought.

"No way, how did you get it?" I was
curious.

"Don't worry about that. Just promise
me that you won't get yourself killed,"
Jholie added.

I instantly thought of Anansi and the
story that Miss Jones told. Could this be
a sign?

"I won't," I assured.

I ran over and jumped on Jholie's
bed. I gave her a hug she couldn't get
away from.

"Let me go, Bri," Jholie complained.

"No, not till you tell me you love
me," I joked.

"I'm gonna call for Mamma," Jholie
said quietly.

I quickly let her go. I threw on my
nightshirt and climbed into my bed. I
pulled the covers over my head. I began to
cry a soft cry, one that only I could
hear. My cries ceased as I grabbed for the
cold metal key that hid my destiny.

CHAPTER 22

Man Overboard

♦ ♦ ♦

Land loomed on the horizon, just a half day away. Mr. Smalls spent the morning corralling his children, Lexi, the eldest and only daughter; Ernest, the eldest son; and Eli, the mischievous youngest, around the ship's hull.

Meanwhile, Mrs. Smalls was in the kitchen with Ruby and Marilyn preparing breakfast when a noise from the washroom caught her attention. Mrs. Smalls handed Ruby a pan and walked down the hall to the washroom where she heard someone moving around. The sound grew clearer, shuffling.

Mrs. Smalls knocked on the door and

the noises stopped. She knocked again and there was nothing, so Mrs. Smalls walked to the kitchen and grabbed a butter knife from a drawer. She returned to the door and began to pry the door open. The lock popped and she slowly opened the door to find Cathy stepping out of the washtub.

"Well, well, well. Thank you cause I sho' was tired of smellin' ya'," Mrs. Smalls smirked.

Cathy grabbed a towel, silent, moving to leave. But Mrs. Smalls blocked the doorway, folding her arms.

"Wasting fresh water, when the sea could've scrubbed ya just as clean."

"Let me by," Cathy muttered, her jaw tight.

"Watch it bitch, you don't own nobody on this ship. On this ship, you are the chattel," Mrs. Smalls mocked a proper accent.

Just then, Eli barreled down the hall, colliding with his mother's side.

"Who's that, Momma?"

"Nobody son," Mrs. Smalls responded.

"Hi, nobody. Bye Nobody," Eli chirped

with a giggle before scampering off.

Cathy, unfazed, sidestepped the distracted Mrs. Smalls and disappeared into her room. Mrs. Smalls returned to the kitchen where she found Eli chewing on a sweet.

She snatched the sweet from Eli who started pouting.

"Breakfast first," she said as the boy's face scrunched with tears.

He bolted out, nearly toppling Mr. Smalls at the doorway. He ran into the legs of Mr. Smalls who leaned down and picked him up.

"What's got you riled?" Mr. Smalls asked, scooping him up.

"Momma took my sweet," Eli explained.

"Well, nah let's see," Mr. Smalls remarked.

Mr. Smalls carried Eli into the kitchen. Mrs. Smalls eyed them both then she walked over to Mr. Smalls. They shared a quick kiss then Mrs. Smalls handed Mr. Smalls a cup of coffee. Mr. Smalls lowered Eli to the floor.

"Don't even ask," said Mrs. Smalls.

"He needs to eat breakfast first."

Mr. Smalls kneeled down with the cup in hand. "You heard your Momma," Mr. Smalls said gently.

"Boy, go tell your brother and sister it's time for breakfast," Mrs. Smalls ordered.

Eli ran down the hall and then above deck.

"Don't bother preparing lunch for me, I'll be deep into planning our dock," Mr. Smalls said.

He turned to Ruby and gave her a signal. She knew exactly what that meant. She scampered out of the kitchen till she was above deck. She grabbed a conch from a rope hanging off the side of the ship. She took a deep breath then blew. Soon after, bodies made their way above deck. All were present except Mr. & Mrs. Smalls and Cathy.

Below deck, Mr. Smalls grabbed Cathy's tray and walked to her door. He knocked. She answered. Mrs. Smalls made her way above deck.

"I'se' gotcha' breakfast," Mr. Smalls

said. Cathy took the tray. "Smells better in here. What did you do?" Mr. Smalls asked.

"I took a bath." Cathy grinned. They shared a laugh.

"I've been thinking a lot about what you asked of me. And as much as I want to, I jus' don't see how we's gon' show up on those lands with you still alive and demanding a baby," Mr. Smalls took a seat.

"I don't know either but least we can try," Cathy responded.

Cathy moved closer to Mr. Smalls who was sitting on her cot. She placed her hand on his back when Eli flung the door open.

"Momma said they waitin' fo' ya', Paw," Eli remarked.

Eli disappeared out of the door but not before he slammed it shut then he jolted above deck. He found his Momma and siblings all standing next to each other.

"Where is your Paw?" Mrs. Smalls questioned.

"He was in the room with Nobody," Eli responded.

"With Nobody?" Marilyn questioned.

"Yeah, you know who," Mrs. Smalls responded.

"His back was itching because Nobody was rubbing it," Eli added.

Mrs. Smalls immediately looked angry. She stomped down below deck. Her stomps became slow, leveled unheard steps. She approached the door and pressed her ear against it. She heard them talking.

"I'll have to talk about this with my Misses," Mr. Smalls said.

"Oh Bobby, you know what she is going to say," Cathy responded.

Mrs. Smalls quickly opened the door. Her mouth flung open.

"Talk to me about what? And who she calling Bobby?"

Mr. Smalls was silent.

"You mean you and this devil bitch have a secret?" Mrs. Smalls said angrily.

Mr. Smalls rose, "No baby, it ain't like that, we were trying to come up with a plan to dock and…" Mr. Smalls tried to explain when he was interrupted.

"And what? Why do you need to talk to

her bout' us docking fo'? What she gots' to do with it? And what Robert Smalls! And what?" she screamed.

"Yan, calm down, nah!" Mr. Smalls said softly.

"Don't tell me to calm down. My husband, the man I love is keeping secrets from me with a white bitch," she cried.

"Yan, it ain't what—"

"Not what?" she snapped. "You scheming with her behind my back?"

"Yan, I was gon' tell you. I jus' didn't know the right time. And I guess this is a good a time as any," Mr. Smalls stood strong.

Mr. Smalls tried to hug Mrs. Smalls but she pulled away.

"Cathy…didn't kill her baby. She left him back at that place we got her from. And now she wants to go back and get the baby," Mr. Smalls explained

Mrs. Smalls walked over to Cathy who looked pitiful and smacked her hard in the face.

"Oh hell no. This bitch is supposed

to be dead," Mrs. Smalls looked at Mr. Smalls with tears in her eyes.

Mr. Smalls looked away.

Her voice cracked as tears welled.

"And you, Bobby? You'd risk us all for her? You is actually considering this?" Mrs. Smalls walks over to Mr. Smalls. "Robert Anthony Smalls answer me!"

Mrs. Smalls demanded.

"Yes, Yan, but this ain't about me caring for her if that is what you mean," Mr. Smalls confessed.

Mrs. Smalls cried out and dropped to the floor. Mr. Smalls dropped down beside her.

"The ways I see it, she can help us dock, Yan. You know an eye for an eye, tooth for a tooth. Just like in those books you like to read."

Mrs. Smalls raised her head.

"Don't try to use the word against me. Did you tell her that you was going back to get that baby?" Mrs. Smalls stood and walked over to Cathy.

"No, I didn't. I was waiting to talk

to you bout' it," Mr. Smalls said.

He reached for Mrs. Smalls again, but she rejected his advances.

"I shoulda' threw your ass over when I had the chance." Mrs. Smalls pointed at Cathy then looked and Mr. Smalls. "And as for you Mr. Smalls, you will not be sleeping in my bed with me tonight or any other night if I can help it."

Mrs. Smalls stood by the cabin door, her expression cold and distant, an echo of the disdain she once reserved for her Mistress. She smoothed her dress, patted her hair, and glanced over her shoulder out of the window to the murky sea. An old swim ritual before jumping into the water. The view of the murky water below deck caused her thoughts to drift slowly, back to childhood, as she remembered the white woman who beat her mother and the love she has for swimming. She snaps back into the moment, face firm and decision final.

"They're waitin' for you above deck," she said, her voice calm but firm. Without another word, she stepped out, leaving Mr. Smalls to follow.

264

Mrs. Smalls walked out and Mr. Smalls followed. They made their way above deck. Mr. Smalls turned and addressed the crowd.

On the deck, a faint breeze swept through the gathered crew as Mr. Smalls addressed them.

"We will be docking come mid-mornin'. Everyone will stay below deck until I send word that it is safe to come above deck.

When we do dock, not a peep out of none of ya'," Mr. Smalls insisted to his crew.

They all nodded and went about their ways. When Lexi, their only daughter let out a scream.

"Momma!" Lexi cried.

All eyes turned. Mrs. Smalls stood at the ship's edge, staring out at the vast expanse of water. Mr. Smalls rushed toward her, his heart sinking.

"Baby, come down from there," he urged cautiously. "You're scarin' the kids."

She turned slowly to face him, her eyes wet but resolute. She glanced at her children, holding each gaze with a painful tenderness.

"I promised myself that no white woman would ever alter my path again. I won't let my kids see it and I won't go through it," she focused on Mr. Smalls.

Mrs. Smalls took a deep breath. While facing her family and with her back to sea, she allowed herself to fall. Screams echoed across the sea. Cries were heard through the crowd. Ruby, hunched over from shock, took the kids below deck.

Mr. Smalls collapsed where he stood, unable to move, until a few crew members steadied him and helped him down to his cabin.

There were no words.

They walked Bobby below deck. He barely used his feet. When they reached his cabin, the men slipped and Mr. Smalls was on his own. Alone now, he pressed his back against the door and released a harrowing, guttural cry. It cut through the ship like a wolf howling to the moon.

They walked closer to Cathy's door. Cathy cracked her door when she heard the commotion. The sight of Mr. Smalls, barely upright between two sailors, stopped her cold.

"What happened?" Cathy questioned.

A younger sailor, JB, locked eyes with her, his gaze hungry. He leaned in and whispered, "Mrs. Smalls jumped."

Bobby let out a wailing cry. Cathy fell against the doorway and gently shut it. The men walked Mr. Smalls into the room and shut the door as they left.

Cathy cracked her door.

The youngest seaman noticed and walked up to Cathy, "I'll be back later," tugging at his britches.

Cathy shut the door then cracked it open to watch the men leave. Later, Cathy crept into Mr. Smalls' room, her steps hesitant. She found him slumped on the edge of the bed, his head heavy with despair.

"Bobby. I am so sorry." She said softly.

Bobby laid still but heard her voice and raised his head. "Get out." He grumbled.

"But Bobby, I jus…" Cathy continued.

"That's Mr. Smalls to you! Get out! Get out!" Bobby interrupted.

"Please, just let me—"

"GET OUT!" he roared, standing unsteadily and shoving her toward the door.

"This is your fault! Her life is on your hands!"

Bobby sees the youngest seaman lingering by Cathy's door but pays him no attention and pulls the door up. The young man wrestled Cathy into her room. Bobby looked away, turned, and walked into his room as if nothing was happening. He tried to ignore it, but he heard Cathy screaming and fighting in the distance. He finally couldn't take it anymore. He rushed through his door then through hers. He wrestled the young seaman off Cathy who was now wearing a black eye and bloody nose.

"What you doing, Cap'n? This white bitch don't mean nothing. We shoulda threw her over like…" The young seamen panted.

Bobby punched the young seamen in the nose. The seaman fell to the floor. Bobby continued to beat on the seaman until the young man wrestled himself free.

"Get out of here and don't come back. When we dock you getting off this here ship for good," Bobby said angrily.

"But Cap'n, you sending me back to slavery if you do that," the young seaman replied.

"I don't want men on my ship like you," Bobby replied.

"What do you mean like me? You agreed to kill a white woman and her baby. Nah you lookin' at me sideways? Can't be," the young seaman fixed his britches.

"Let him stay, I ain't hurt none. It's just a little blood," Cathy interjected.

"Oh, so nah you the Cap'n?" The young seaman looked at Cathy.

"Get out, JB, I'll talk to youlater," Bobby pointed at the door.

JB glared but slinked out of the cabin, slamming the door behind him.

Bobby turned to Cathy, his expression a storm of anger and regret. Without a word, he stumbled from her room and disappeared into his own. Cathy sat alone, her body trembling as guilt coursed through her. She hugged herself tightly, staring at the floor, the silence broken only by the quiet drip of her tears.

CHAPTER 23

The Deal

♦ ♦ ♦

The morning arrived heavy with grief. Though the crew moved quietly, mourning weighed on their faces as they followed Bobby's orders without hearing a word from him. The eldest seaman dropped anchor at a bustling port, crowded with seven other ships, all operated by white captains.

From the deck, he squinted at a nearby vessel and frowned in recognition. It was the same ship they'd crossed paths with a few days earlier. The captain of the other ship took notice of them, too.

The captain of the neighboring vessel, a burly white man with a weathered face, called out, "Ahoy there, nigga!

Where's your captain?" The old seaman gestured with one finger, then shuffled down, below deck, and wrapped on Bobby's door.

"Cap'n we gots' ourselves a problem," said the old seaman. Bobby slowly rose to acknowledge the old seaman's presence.

"Memba' that ship we ran into days back? Well, they right next to us and theys' Cap'n asking to see ours," the old seaman explained.

Bobby looked worried. He got dressed.

"And theys' spectin' to see a White man," the old seaman added.

Bobby sighed heavily. Without a word, he made his way to Cathy's door. He hesitated before knocking but knew there was no other way to salvage this situation. Cathy, startled by the knock, remained still until she heard Bobby's voice.

"It's me," Bobby whispered.

Cathy recognized his voice and opened the door fully dressed with her hair pulled up. Bobby pushed into her room.

"Listen Cathy we's got trouble. We

need to dock to collect supplies but that old ship we seen out at sea is right next to us. Nah, they are spectin' to see a white man. Will you help us? We been through enough already. Please!" Bobby begged.

Cathy walked off and sat on her cot.

"Look, I'll set you free when this is over. You can get someone to help you find your baby—"

"There's no one," Cathy interrupted. Her voice cracked. "Just you. Help me, and I'll help you."

Bobby began to pace back and forth. He knew what he had to do but he didn't like it at all. It reminded him of the manipulation that slave masters used on their slaves.

"Fine, but you follow my words and not the other way round'," Bobby replied.

On impulse, she reached out to embrace Bobby, but he stepped back, pushing her hand away.

"Start by dealin' with that captain," Bobby instructed.

Cathy adjusted her dress and walked above deck with a newfound resolve.

"Hey, not you again. I'd swear that you are following us," Cathy remarked.

The white captain removed his hat and covered his chest with it.

"Nah Mam, I am not. Where's your mister?" The white captain questioned.

Her face crumpled, and tears welled in her eyes.

"He fell ill and passed," she whispered, her voice trembling.

"Oh, I am sorry to hear that, Mam. Are you okay? I mean on board with all those niggers," he asked, lowering his voice conspiratorially.

Cathy bit her lip, glancing over her shoulder.

"I manage," she said, forcing a smile. Then, raising her voice, she called to the crew, "Prepare for docking!"

Everyone looked confused until they saw Mr. Smalls walk out and drop the ladder that connected to the dock.

"Well, Mam looks like you gon' need some help. Let me show you where to get some rations and supplies. You leaving soon?" The white captain asked.

"Yeah, in a few days. Let me talk to these niggers and get them settled, you know how they can be," Cathy remarked.

She disappeared below deck with Bobby following close behind. They stop at the bottom of the steps.

"Niggas?" Bobby wiped his face in relief.

"I had to make it believable. You just remember what you promised," Cathy said.

"I ain't forgot," Bobby replied.

"Now how am I supposed to get rid of him," Cathy asked.

"Oh no, don't get rid of him, let him take you to get some supplies. I'll send Ruby to go with you then we can have the seamen pick it up. Act like you can't pay for it, too."

A look of sarcasm brushed over Cathy's face.

"What about JB, can we trust him?" Cathy asked.

"Don't worry about him, I will deal

with that. Just go and act believable. If
you ain't back by midday, I am leaving
without cha'," Bobby warned.

Cathy looked at Bobby then walked up
the steps.

"I'll be back," Cathy assured Mr.
Smalls. "Don't leave."

She made her way down the ramp onto
land. The white captain stood waiting,
holding out his arm. Cathy took his arm
and they walked off.

Bobby and the oldest seaman emerged
above deck.

"You think she coming back Cap'n?"
The old seaman questioned.

"Yeah, she'll be back," Bobby said
confidently.

"How you know?" the Old seaman
questioned.

"I just do," Bobby replied. "I'm
gonna go check on my children. They need
me right nah."

Without another word, they both
disappeared below deck.

CHAPTER 24

An Eye for a Lie

The next morning, I found myself at Mr. Stone's cottage, determined to make him see that my plan involving Sara was his best option. I marched up to the door, but before I could knock, a faint cry echoed from the woods. A baby's cry.

I knew that it had to be Mr. Stone. I followed the sound of the cry, but something wasn't right. It felt like I was being followed, so I quickly looked over my shoulder, but there was no one. I even looked up into the trees to see if Jholie was snooping around.

I found Mr. Stone's carriage near the shallow part of the river where the trees bend funny. He wasn't expecting to see me.

I could tell by the way his eyes rolled up in his head when he saw me.

"What nah girl?" he grumbled.

"I found a way to help you," I said with care.

"Did I ask you for any help?" His tone was sharp, almost dismissive.

"No, but you need it. That baby gone need a Momma," I replied, stepping closer to the carriage.

Mr. Stone scoffed, arms folded.

"How you know what a baby need. I done raised a chile' without a woman round'," Mr. Stone said with confidence.

I peered into the carriage. The baby lay bundled and sleeping peacefully, its tiny face smooth and serene.

I turned back to Mr. Stone.

"At least hear me out," I urged.

From behind a tree, not too far from where we were, stepped Sara. Mr. Stone saw her before I did. He turned around and sat on a tree stump.

"Please tell me this ain't your plan," he said, voice laced with disappointment.

"Just hear me out," I continued.

Sara moved closer to us. She kept her eyes on Mr. Stone.

"Stoney, I'm sorry," Sara started to speak.

"Too late, nah," he cut in, his tone sharp.

"It ain't never too late, Stoney," Sara persisted, her voice carrying an urgency that matched the tears forming in her eyes.

"It's been sixteen years," he snapped, the words cutting through the still air like a blade.

Standing there, watching them, pieces began to fall into place. I remembered how Meema had said Sara was sad back then, though she'd never explained why. The memory twisted in my mind alongside every conversation I'd had with Sara, her talk of a man and children. Could she be Brik's mama? Did Brik even know? My heart raced with questions I wasn't sure I wanted answered.

"You left me alone to raise a boy, who needed his Momma," Mr. Stone said, voice rising with years of pent-up anger. Sara walked over to Mr. Stone and kneeled down in front of him.

Sara dropped to her knees before him.

"I didn't know what to do…after. I'm sorry, Stoney. I'm here now, and I want to make it right. With you. With Brik," Sara pleaded.

"That boy don't even know—," his voice broke off, and he looked at me suddenly. His eyes narrowed.

I stared back at him.

"You know everything nah don'tcha'." Mr. Stone snapped at me.

"It ain't like that—" I started.

"You what? You betta' not tell Brik nothing you heard here. Let me handle it,"

Mr. Stone interrupted.

"I won't. I promise," I said quickly, crossing my heart with my finger and pointing to the sky.

"Since we all here, because you had to go and stick your big nose in my biness', what is the plan?" Mr. Stone asked.

I walked over closer to them. "The

way I see it, Sara can walk around for a while with pillows stuffed in her front so that it looks like she is having a baby.

Meema says some women don't show at all, right up until it's time. And in a little while, you can act like you pushed the baby out. I will help you keep that a…secret," I hesitated then thought.

"In order for this to work, I'm gone have to move back in with you Stoney. That will help make it believable," Sara added,

"You tired of sleeping with the horses, huh? I guess," Mr. Stone huffed.

"Look, if you gonna be like that, I don't have to do this Stoney. But you should think about the life this child is gonna have," Sara remarked.

"Did you think about the life Brik was gonna have?" Mr. Stone quickly responded.

"I said I'm sorry Stoney, what more do you want? My mind left me, but it's back now and I'm better," Sara admitted.

"How do I know that?" Mr. Stone was skeptical.

"You don't! You just have to trust

me," Sara added.

"Easier said than done, but…" Mr. Stone stood and faced Sara.

His facial expression changed. He stood, thinking. "It would help me get back to work. The sky is about to change and I got a lot of chopping to do.

Everyone gon' need firewood."

Mr. Stone paused and walked to the edge of the river but quickly returned to the carriage.

"Well, we can try this, for the child's sake, under one condition…Sara you gone have to give it up," Mr. Stone and I looked at Sara.

Sara smiled.

She knew exactly what we were talking about. I held my hand out. Sara pulled out her flask and took a long swig. She acted as if she was going to place it in my hands but she gave it another shake. You could hear the drops of liquid sloshing back and forth inside the flask. Sara put the flask to her mouth and turned it upside down one last time. She stared compassionately at the flask.

"I'm gonna miss you," she said. Sara placed her old flask in my hand.

"Okay, just for a while," Sara added.

"For good!" I replied.

I threw the flask deep into the river's eye. Sara and Mr. Stone gave each other a hug that seemed long overdue.

"I missed you," Mr. Stone whispered.

"I'm sorry," Sara apologized.

Mr. Stone grabbed Sara's hands and walked her over to the carriage. She peeked in. She immediately started to cry then turned away from the carriage. Mr. Stone walked over and hugged her from behind.

"He looks just like…" Sara started to say.

"I know, I know. You'll do just fine. This here will be like your second chance," Mr. Stone said softly.

She used Mr. Stone's shoulder to hoist herself into the back of the carriage. Mr. Stone hoisted himself up top. They rode off towards Mr. Stone's cottage.

◆ ◆ ◆

When they reached the cottage, Mr. Stone rode up to the back door.

Brik heard the cart from inside and met him at the door like usual except this time was different.

"Daddy…Hello Miss Sara," Brik greeted.

They both get out of the cart, Sara holding the baby. Brik helped Sara up the steps.

"Hello Brik, boy how you've grown," Sara sighed.

Sara walked through the door of a home that she once knew. The cottage was well lit by evenly placed hand-made sconces on the walls. Up against the main wall in the living quarters stood a grand fireplace made of cobblestone. The doors of each bedroom were made from burl wood. Sara walked over and picked up a small decorative box.

She opened the box. A tune was heard and a clown, holding red balloons popped up and began to spin around in a circular motion. Sara looked back at Mr. Stone. Mr. Stone put his finger over his mouth in a shushing motion then he walked over to Brik.

"She gon' be helping us with the...well you know, for a while and we gots'ta' keep this a secret. Sara gon' walk around and act like she expectin' for a while and then..."

Brik stared hard at his Daddy. A look of awe covered his face.

"Daddy why? We doing fine just by ourselves," Brik whispered.

"I know but what you think gonna happen when this here chile' gets big and wants to go play with the other chillen? You gonna be the one to tell'em' no. Cause I never could," Mr. Stone remarked.

Brik took a step away from his Daddy and then came back up to him.

"Daddy, you sure this is going to work?" Brik whispered.

"I hope so, for the child's sake," Mr. Stone said. Brik took the baby from Sara. He lays him in his bassinet. Sara and Mr. Stone walked into his bedroom.

"So you gonna tell me how you got this baby, Stoney?" Sara asked.

"Do we got to talk about it nah?" Mr. Stone replied.

"No, but we gon' talk about it, but first you gon' sit your butt down in this here tub. I'll grab your razor and start boiling the water," Sara insisted.

Mr. Stone looked at Sara. Although he was a sure man, he felt a little unsure about this situation. In a way, he was happy she'd returned but worried about Brik. There was so much that he needed to explain and he didn't know where to start. All that he did know was that Brik needed to hear it from him and no one else.

Sara prepared the bath and gave Mr. Stone a shave. He emerged from his bath unrecognizable. The odor that became his shadow had vanished. He was clean. All of a sudden, there was a hard, fast knocking on the bedroom door. When it opened, Brik had to look his Daddy up and down. He almost didn't recognize him.

"Daddy come quick, it's Bri's grandma, Meema, she ain't doing too good, they say she ain't got long. I gotsta' go help find Bri," Brik dashed away.

"Oh, my, my. Let me get on over there and check on Baybruh. Sara, please look after Rok, I mean…the baby."

"No, you mean Rok," Sara replied. "I got him."

Sara nodded then sat in the rocker on the porch. Mr. Stone grabbed his hat and headed over to check on Meema.

CHAPTER 25

Troubles of the World

After speaking with Sara and Mr. Stone, I spent the rest of the day riding with Bam. It had been a while since she'd mounted a horse, and I could see how much she'd missed it. Her posture softened as we took our familiar route through the woods, passing the old schoolhouse, our childhood echoing faintly in the distance. When we reached the cornfield, we paused for a while, the silence between us filled with memories.

"So tell me, how has it been, Momma?" I ventured, breaking the quiet.

Bam exhaled, her breath carrying the weight of motherhood.

"It's been okay I guess, I don't how

else it's supposed to be," Bam replied.

She turned to me with a small grin.

"And what about you, Mrs. Brik Stone?"

"Bam, don't play with me," I said, brushing it off, but I could feel the heat rise in my cheeks.

"You know that boy is crazy bout' you. Why won't you give him a chance?" Bam asked.

"Why? So, I can end up like you." The words escaped before I could stop them, sharp and unintended.

Bam stiffened, and her smile faded.

"What do you mean like me, Bri?"

There was an edge to her voice, and I knew this could turn ugly if I wasn't careful.

"Nothing, Bam…"

"Oh, it's something," she wasn't letting this go.

"Well you know we made plans and you ruined them. You left me on my own," I said.

Bam's eyes darkened with hurt, but she held her ground.

"Still selfish. You know after all
this time and everything that we've been
through, I thought you'd changed, but you
really haven't," Bam frowned.

"I *have* changed." I straightened in
the saddle, defiance in my tone. "I know
more now than ever what I'm gonna do with
myself and it ain't being no Momma or no
wife," I said with confidence.

Bam's expression softened, and her
voice turned quiet but firm.

"Bri ain't nothing wrong with being a
Momma or wife."

Bam walked over to Bri with a smile
on her face.

"Cause guess what happens after
that?... You get to be a Meema."

I looked at Bam and felt everything
that she had said. Those words struck me
harder than I expected. I felt their
weight settle into the quiet parts of my
heart. Meema's face flashed in my mind,
warm and wise. She'd always known just
what to say, and for a moment, I wanted to
argue, but I couldn't.

We hugged then, tighter than we had in years. It wasn't just affection; it was forgiveness. Mounting our horses, we turned toward the stables. But as we neared, Jholie came running, her face streaked with dirt and tears

"What is it Jholie. And don't use Meema as an excuse this time, cause it won't work!" I hopped down and turned my back on Jholie to adjust my saddle.

Jholie panted, barely able to speak.

"It's... it's Meema," she gasped.

"You've gotta come. Quick!"

"Jholie I have no time for this," I said frustrated.

"I am serious Bri," Jholie bent over.

The look in her eyes told me everything. Without another word, I mounted, pulling Jholie up behind me. We rode hard, the horses galloping as if they too understood the urgency.

When we reached the house, I leaped off before Hadie had fully stopped. Jholie tumbled to the ground, but I didn't turn back. I knew this had to be serious because a crowd started to gather. I slammed through the door and there she was, Meema, lying so still, Mamma and Deddy kneeling by her bedside.

The room smelled of lavender, her favorite.

"Meema," I said gently. I couldn't hold back the tears.

"Fix your face, nah, girl," she said, her voice still carrying its signature strength.

She beckoned for me to come closer. I walked over to her and leaned down close to her. She was barely breathing and her skin felt cold as ice. She whispered something just for me, soft and fleeting before taking one last breath.

And just like that, she was gone.

"Meema, Meema, Meema," my voice cracked as I shook her gently, refusing to accept it.

Bam pulled me away, holding me tight as I wept against her shoulder. The world outside seemed unreal, but the pain in my chest was sharp and real.

Deddy stumbled out onto the porch,

collapsing to the ground, his grief raw and unrestrained. Mr. Stone came and helped him into a chair. Mamma followed, but her face was an empty mask, her eyes dull and distant.

That night, we all felt numb and no one said a word.

The next few days were a blur then the morning of Meema's last ride came. Deddy was having a hard time, but it seemed like Mamma was taking it the hardest. Deddy had to make the day's mark in her stick. Mamma barely wanted to get out of bed. She was supposed to be responsible for getting Meema ready for her last ride, but she couldn't bring herself to it. The other elder ladies chipped in including Bam's Momma, Betty, and Cousin Sherry.

Meema was a natural woman. She loved everything about nature. I can remember a conversation that she had with Deddy a long time ago. Deddy wasn't interested in having the conversation at all, but Meema made him sit and listen. She told him the time will come when she would no longer breathe and that he had to be strong for the rest of the family. She told him to place her naked body in the ground without a box so that she could make the corn grow. Although he was reluctant at first, he agreed.

The walk to the Praise House was the heaviest I'd ever known. Deddy saddled two albino horses to our best carriage where Meema's body was placed on a bed of roses that Mamma and Sara had sewn and decorated. Slope's best singers sang some of the elders to the ground as the lead singer slowly walked behind the carriage singing, *Trouble of the World*.

"Soon I will be gone
No mo'e troubles of the world No
mo'e troubles of the world No mo'e
troubles! of the world

Soon I will be gone
No mo'e troubles! of the world
Going home! to live! with God! No
mo'e! weapin unwilling
No more! weapin unwilling No more!
weapin unwilling

Going home! to live! with my lord!

Soon I will be gone
No mo'e troubles of the world No
mo'e troubles of the world
No mo'e troubles! of the world

Soon I will be gone
No mo'e trouble! of the world Going
home! to live! with my lord!

I want! see my motha
I want! to see my motha I want! to
see my motha
Going home! to live with God!
Soon we will be gone
No mo'e troubles of the world No
mo'e troubles of the world No mo'e
troubles! of the world

I'll soon, will be done! With the
trouble of the world
I'm going home to live! with God!"
The carriage finally reached the
Praise House. Deddy, Linc, Mr. Stone,
Brik, and Gene helped to get Meema's body

off the carriage and into the Praise House. Meema's body was mounted on a stand while everyone was seated.

The Praiser approached the podium and let out a rhythmic moan. Everyone followed suit. I bowed my head and began to hum too. I felt something rise in me, a heat, a trembling, a grief too vast to hold. I started feeling hot. My palms started sweating and my body started to tremble. Before you knew it my face was full of tears. It's weird because I don't remember this next part. Jholie filled me in later on in the day.

She said that I yelled out Meema's name over and over again until I passed out. When I came to, we were riding in the back of Mr. Stone's carriage on the way to the burial. Jholie said I looked like a fish without water, but some said the spirit got into me. That is exactly what Meema would have said. Maybe it was Meema. She was really the only one who knew my doubts when it came to spirits.

We buried her in the empty lot closest to the cornfields. Brik sectioned it off with a wooden fence he painted yellow. Mr. Stone made her a block on which he carved the following epitaph: *Here lies "Meema" The Creator's Gift to Slope. Queen of Slope.* Sara decorated her block with the prettiest of flowers.

Everyone was shocked to see Sara and Mr. Stone together, again, but nothing was ever the same. Every seventh notch, Mamma and Deddy rode over to the side of the cornfield where Meema was buried to decorate the grave with fresh flowers. Sometimes I found myself riding there too just to have one of our talks.

On her deathbed, she told me to find my future and never fear the unknown. She said that my strength should come from me being a woman and don't be afraid to use it to my advantage. She also told me to use that key.

It was time.

That was just like her. Although she didn't mention it till now, she always wanted me to know. I plan to act on her words for the rest of my days.

Epilogue

With the key in hand, one thing left to do
Find the lock-in which this dark key fits
Decision has been made, no doubt exists
Should I reassemble the last old crew?

Find new members is that the thing to do?
I could go at this alone, I could quit
I was destined to know, my life's commit
Fear didn't matter, truth long overdue

Like lit puzzle pieces, I found my way
Every step was a bit clearer to me
I just happened to find love on the go

It was in the words that he used to say
Too bad that Meema didn't live to see The
seeds that I would one day learn to sow.

Acknowledgment

This book began as a thought I had in 2009. The narrative surrounding the process by which enslaved people were acquired and portrayed as complacent and content never sat well with me. I couldn't shake the feeling that there must be other untold stories—stories that didn't conform to that narrative. But a significant question loomed: when, where, and how would these stories be written for future generations to explore and learn?

Determined to take action, I decided to put my thoughts down on paper. I knew I might never be able to prove the validity of the words I was writing, but evidence wasn't my ultimate goal. My aim was to ignite young minds, to inspire them to think critically about our history, our history, full of stolen fighters, brilliant scientists, and meticulous timekeepers. I hoped to spark the realization that by working together, supporting one another, and embracing our shared greatness, we can all thrive and leave a lasting legacy.

More recently, I was inspired again by a docuseries titled *Enslaved*, which deeply explored the origins and mechanisms of the transatlantic slave trade. Watching the series reignited my passion and ideas, leading me to construct a screenplay for what would become my book series, *Blood Ships*.

About The Author

Ms. Amy Blackwell was born on an Army base in Fort Belvoir, Virginia, and raised in St. Louis, Missouri. From a young age, she developed a deep love for reading and writing, passions that would shape her life and career. As a proud graduate of the University City Public School District, she credits her early education with fostering her resilience, problem-solving abilities, and determination.

Ms. Blackwell has pursued an impressive academic journey, earning multiple degrees that reflect her dedication to education. She holds a Bachelor of Arts in English with an emphasis in Creative Writing from Webster University, a Bachelor of Science in Secondary Education with an English emphasis from Harris-Stowe State

University, and a Master's degree in Educational Administration from Lindenwood University. Additionally, she achieved certification as a Reading Specialist through a Special Reading certificate program.

Currently, this accomplished Black educator is completing a Doctorate in Educational Leadership at Maryville University, which she anticipates earning in May 2021. With her extensive expertise and passion for teaching, Ms. Blackwell now inspires young minds as an English Language Arts teacher for freshmen in a high school located in St. Louis's North County.

www.ingramcontent.com/pod-product-compliance
Lightning Source LLC
Chambersburg PA
CBHW060406260626
47160CB00006B/2453